Tim Bowler

OXFORD
UNIVERSITY PRESS

# OXFORD
## UNIVERSITY PRESS

Great Clarendon Street, Oxford OX2 6DP
Oxford University Press is a department of the University of Oxford.
It furthers the University's objective of excellence in research, scholarship,
and education by publishing worldwide in

Oxford New York

Auckland Cape Town Dar es Salaam Hong Kong Karachi
Kuala Lumpur Madrid Melbourne Mexico City Nairobi
New Delhi Shanghai Taipei Toronto

With offices in

Argentina Austria Brazil Chile Czech Republic France Greece
Guatemala Hungary Italy Japan Poland Portugal Singapore
South Korea Switzerland Thailand Turkey Ukraine Vietnam

Oxford is a registered trade mark of Oxford University Press
in the UK and in certain other countries

First published 2013
First published in paperback 2014

British Library Cataloguing in Publication Data

Data available

ISBN: 978-0-19-272870-8
1 3 5 7 9 10 8 6 4 2

Printed in Great Britain
Paper used in the production of this book is a natural,
recyclable product made from wood grown in sustainable forests.
The manufacturing process conforms to the environmental
regulations of the country of origin.

*For Elizabeth, for Doreen, and for Rachel*

*'We have lingered in the chambers of the sea'*
T. S. Eliot

# *Chapter 1*

They told her she was a dreamer, that the pictures she saw were an illusion, that sea glass could not tell a story; but this was a different kind of story. Its thread had been snapped so long ago she had no memory of it, yet the effects had haunted her ever since; and now, fourteen years later, her life was to change again. She'd sensed it already in the whispers from the sea; and here was a new manifestation.

'You must be able to see it, Tam,' she said.

He didn't answer. He just sat there next to her on the cliff-top, staring at the sea glass in her hand. She turned her head and gazed about her: nothing moved on the rocky bluff and a heavy silence hung over the island. She thought of the others down in the bay and wondered why she couldn't hear them. She felt sure their voices should reach her in this windless calm. She turned back to Tam and saw him watching her face.

'You're meant to be looking at the sea glass,' she said.

'I can't see anything in it, Hetty.'

'I'll hold it higher.'

She raised the sea glass. It looked dull against the bleak October sky, especially now that the light was fading, but the image was still there: a dark shape floating in the glass, as though breathed there by the sea.

'Can you see it now?' she said.

But he was looking at her again.

1

'Tam, it's important.'

'I won't see anything,' he said. 'I never do.'

'But the sea glass was blank a moment ago and now it's got a picture inside it.'

He peered at it again, but she knew he was feigning interest. She lowered the sea glass and closed it inside her hand. He glanced round at her.

'I haven't finished looking.'

'Never mind,' she said. 'You're right. You're never going to see anything. Nobody ever does.' She frowned. 'I'm the only crazy person on Mora.'

Tam pulled his knees into his chest.

'So what's the picture this time? Or are you going to keep it to yourself? You've got really funny about the sea glass lately. You used to tell me everything.'

She leaned closer to him.

'I thought I saw the island in it.'

'This island?'

'Of course this island.' She gave him an impatient look. 'What other island would I be talking about?'

'You might have meant one of the others.'

'How could I recognize islands I've never been to?'

'You know what they all look like. My father's described them to you enough times.'

'I meant this island,' she said.

'But how could you tell it was Mora in the sea glass?'

'The top was shaped like North Point,' she said, 'and there were bits that looked like Scar Cliff and Holm Edge and High Crag and . . .'

She stopped suddenly.

'What's wrong?' said Tam.

'I don't want you to laugh at me over the sea glass.'

'I'm not going to laugh at you.'

'Other people do.'

2

'I'm not other people, Hetty. You know that.'

He had that expression on his face again: the one that had only started appearing since they turned fifteen. She still wasn't sure what to do about it. All she knew was that it made her feel awkward—and somehow guilty. She looked down at the ground.

'It's not Mora in the sea glass, Tam.'

'You just said you saw the island.'

'I said I thought I did. But I was wrong. The picture started out looking like Mora, but then it changed.'

'Into what?'

'Doesn't matter.' She flicked a small stone over the edge of the cliff, then thrust the sea glass into her pocket. 'Let's drop it.'

She turned her head and stared down from the cliff-top. The water below looked steely and still. She ran her eye over the rocky bar that stretched across the mouth of the bay as far as Eel Point. The giant boulders that guarded the anchorage had no work to do in this interminable calm: the sea was unruffled all the way to the horizon. She glanced at *The Pride of Mora*, sitting at her mooring. The island boat was bedecked with bunting but all the flags hung limp.

'Looks like most people have arrived,' said Tam, staring down too.

Hetty looked over the shingle beach. It was crawling with figures. She searched for the spot where she'd found the sea glass that morning and saw Mungo and Duffy splashing stones there with Nessa and Jinty just behind them. Tam's mother and father wandered past with Anna and Dolly and some of the families from the western cottages. A large crowd had already gathered near the top of the beach.

Tam started counting the figures aloud. Hetty pushed the sound of his voice away and squeezed the sea glass

3

in her pocket, her mind on the image within, and on the stillness of the water below; there was something about it that didn't feel right.

'The whole island's turned out,' said Tam eventually. 'Mother said they would. Come on. We'd better get down there.'

He jumped to his feet and reached a hand down to pull her up. She pretended not to see it and scrambled up by herself.

'Tam, listen,' she said, 'you go on ahead, all right?'

'What for?'

'I want to take my time going down.'

'You mean you want to be on your own.'

'I didn't say that.'

'Have I upset you over the sea glass?'

'No, of course not.' She glanced over at the darkening sea, then back at Tam. 'I just want a bit of time to think, all right?'

He shrugged.

'If you say so. But don't take too long or you'll miss Per's speech.'

'I was half-hoping I would.'

'You mustn't, Hetty. You know that. We both mustn't. My mother and father gave me a lecture about it. And you must have got one from Grandy.'

Hetty remembered her grandmother's words over breakfast.

'I don't want to hear the old buzzard's speech either, girl, but he's the oldest person on Mora and the only one to make it to a hundred, so we've both got to be at the party and that's that. And try not to look bored when the old boy pipes up. I know you don't like each other, but it's his big day and if you can't celebrate that, then think of *The Pride of Mora* and remember it's her birthday too.

4

And she really is something worth celebrating. Now go and tidy your room.'

'I'll see you down there,' said Tam, and he ran off down the path.

Hetty waited till he'd disappeared from view, then made her way down to the plateau of Broken Tooth Ridge. The bay below her was growing darker by the minute but lights were now moving over the beach, and at the top of the shingle, where the dinghies and small craft had been pulled beyond the tidemark, she could see a fire burning and figures packed around it. The smell of roasting meat wafted up to her.

She felt in her pocket for the sea glass again, thinking of the image swimming inside it, and of the other images, the ones that had never come, in spite of her years of searching; and she thought of the sea again, and the secrets it was keeping from her. The figures on the beach were more shadowy now, but the groupings were so familiar she could still see who was who.

Old Per was standing with Gregor, Harold, and his other codger friends, plus Lorna and some of the older women, though not Grandy, Anna, or Dolly; they were busy with the fire. Tam was larking about with Mungo, Duffy, and the girls, and some of the gang from North Point. She walked on down the path and didn't stop till she'd reached the little quay tucked into the edge of the bay.

The voices of the others were audible now and it was clear that the speeches had not yet started. She stared over at the figures by the fire, then on an impulse wandered down to the end of the landing stage, pulled out the sea glass, and searched again for the image she had seen inside it. She felt sure it would not be there: the pictures never stayed for long, and some vanished within seconds. Yet to her surprise, it was still visible, even in the darkness:

not a picture of Mora as she had first thought, but of a face peering back at her. She heard a whisper from the sea and looked up.

Nothing moved upon the water. She stared about her, shivering slightly. Over to the right, the shingle beach curved away into the shoulder of the cliff, the fire crackling halfway along it. To her left, all was still. No waves lapped against the base of Crab Rock at the eastern extremity of the land. Ahead of her, the mouth of the bay opened to the approaching night. A light swell passed through it and died on the boulders of Eel Point. *The Pride of Mora* did not stir. Hetty squeezed the sea glass again.

'It's starting,' she murmured.

# Chapter 2

By the time the speeches were announced, darkness had
tightened its grip upon the bay. Hetty stared up at the sky.
It was a moonless, starless vault that seemed to mirror
the blackness of the sea. All that illumined the beach was
the fire blazing at the top where most of the people were
gathered. Some, however, had wandered off down the
shingle, and Gregor was now summoning them back in
his high, peppery voice.

But there were other voices too, and Hetty listened to
them all: chattery voices, raucous voices, nervous voices.
Some were slurred and had a hint of defiance in them, and
she knew that though the food had all been eaten, there
would be a number of people who were in no hurry for
the speeches to start while there was still brew to drink.

For her part, she just wished she could run home to
Moon Cottage. She waited at the back and let others push
forward to where Per was standing on the upturned hull
of his dinghy, his face lit by the glow of the fire. Lorna,
Harold and Per's other old friends stood nearby, apart
from Gregor who was still hobbling about the beach trying to muster the truants.

'Hetty,' said a voice.

She looked round and saw her grandmother watching
her.

'Thought so,' said Grandy.

'What did you think?'

'That you'd be hanging round here at the back of the crowd.'

'I turned up, though, Grandy, didn't I?'

'You did, girl. Well done.'

Mackie lumbered over, looking anxious.

'Something wrong, big man?' said Grandy.

'Isla says Tam's disappeared.'

'Don't tell me you've lost your son again.'

'It's no joke, Grandy,' said Mackie. 'We're really worried about him. He's been acting so strange this last year. He's a good lad but we never know what's going on in his head these days. And he's getting reckless too.'

'You were reckless when you were his age.'

Mackie took no notice of this and turned to Hetty.

'Have you seen him, girl? He's usually with you. Or looking for you.'

'We were up on the cliff-top,' said Hetty, 'but he came down ahead of me. I saw him on the beach on my way down, but I don't know where he is now.'

'I'm here,' said Tam from behind them.

He squeezed quickly between her and Mackie.

'Where the hell have you been?' said Mackie. 'I told you to be here for the speeches.'

'And I am,' said Tam. 'They haven't started yet.'

'They're about to.'

Tam glanced at the crowd gathering around Per, then back at Mackie.

'Sorry, Father,' he said.

'So where were you?'

'With Mungo. He was trying to climb Crab Rock.'

'What!'

'And he fell off. But he was only about a quarter of the way up, so he hasn't hurt himself. He's over there with Duffy and the others.'

Mackie shook his head.

'That's stupid even by Mungo's standards. Crab Rock's far too dangerous for climbing. I don't know what's got into you and your crowd. You turn fifteen and it's like you all lose your brains.'

'You climbed Crab Rock when you were fifteen,' said Grandy quietly.

Mackie glowered at her.

'You did,' she said.

He grunted.

'I'm almost wanting the speeches to start, Grandy,' he muttered, 'if that's what it takes to shut you up.'

And they both chuckled. But the speeches were at last starting. Gregor was now standing next to Per on the upturned dinghy and the crowd appeared to be settling down. Hetty scanned the figures in front of her. Mungo, Duffy, Nessa, and Jinty were down to the right, sniggering over some private joke, but they broke apart as she watched and slipped away to join their families in the crowd. Mungo caught her eye and gave a goofy smile.

'Let's get closer, girl,' said Grandy.

'I can see from here.'

'Well, I can't,' said Grandy, 'and I can't hear as good as you either.'

They edged into the back of the crowd, Grandy holding her by the arm. She felt Tam move with her, a little closer than she wanted, but she said nothing. Isla joined them, exchanged a few words with Mackie, then cuffed Tam round the head. Gregor cleared his throat.

'Well, now,' he said, 'it's not often we get the whole island together like this, not often enough, in my view, and I'm sorry it's me you got to listen to first. God knows I ain't no speaker—'

'I'll second that!' someone shouted.

A burst of laughter rippled round the group. Gregor managed a smile.

'But it's fallen to me,' he went on, 'to start things off, seeing as I'm the second most ancient person on Mora.' He glanced at Per, standing rigidly beside him, then at Lorna. 'And seeing as the third most ancient person says she don't want to do no talking tonight.'

'She ain't been that quiet in ninety years,' put in Harold.

'And I don't suppose it'll last,' said Gregor, 'but we live in hope.'

'Get on with it,' muttered Lorna.

More laughter greeted this exchange, and some light-hearted heckling. Per remained silent, immobile. Hetty studied the old man's face in the fluctuating light from the fire. Even in the darkness and with so many others in front of her, she was convinced that his eyes were seeking hers. She thought of their quarrels down the years and squeezed the sea glass in her pocket; and as she did so, her mind moved back to the image within it, and to the sea whispering behind her.

'Like I say,' Gregor continued, 'we don't often get to-gether like this, but we got two good reasons tonight, don't we? To celebrate two great servants of our commu-nity. So let's start off with *The Pride of Mora*.'

This brought forth a cheer and a turning of heads to survey the island boat.

'Our beautiful little ship,' said Gregor, 'and sweeter than ever now Mackie and his crew have made her a new set of sails. I still can't believe she's fifty years old. But that ain't nothing compared to our other great servant.'

And he turned towards Per, still standing impassively beside him.

'Hundred years old today,' said Gregor, 'and I can't believe that neither, old friend. And I don't doubt no one else can. But we all salute you.'

He turned back to the group.

'Let's hear it for old Per!'

And he started a handclap. Per's friends joined in at once, then others, and gradually the applause spread round the whole group, only to stop with a strange abruptness, leaving an edgy silence. Gregor stepped off the dinghy and Hetty waited, aware of the whispering sea again, and the tension in the listeners. Per looked them over for some time, apparently in no hurry to speak.

'Well, well,' he said eventually, 'it's kind of you all to come and celebrate my birthday.' He took a slow breath. 'Even if it's only out of duty for most of you.'

Hetty felt the tension deepen. Again Per watched them in silence for a while, then he gave a chuckle and turned towards *The Pride of Mora*.

'Only it don't seem fair I got to share a birthday with her,' he said. 'I'm only going to come off worse. She's half my age and twice as good looking.'

No one laughed. Not even Gregor.

'But there you go,' said Per. 'No one said life was just.'

The old man's eyes flickered over his audience again.

'Gregor's right, though,' he went on. '*The Pride*'s a beautiful little ship. I remember building her all them years ago, shaping her keel and her ribs and her masts, making her first set of wings. Labour of love for me, that was.'

'Only it wasn't just you, Per,' called Mackie. 'Wasn't just you built *The Pride*.'

'No, Mackie, it wasn't,' Per retorted. 'Gregor and Harold and my other old friends done their part too.'

'And my father,' shouted Mackie, 'and Rory's father and Karl's father and Hal's father, and others no longer with us, God rest 'em.'

'I never said they done nothing,' Per spluttered, 'but those of us what was there at the time know who done the lion's share and who didn't. And you can't gainsay that, Mackie, because you wasn't even born!'

A buzz of talk ran round the group.

'Stop that now!' Per thundered. 'You're getting worked up over the wrong thing. I ain't here to argue about the past. I'm here to warn you about the future. Because we got something far more important to worry about right now.'

'Change your tune, old man,' called Rory.

'That's right,' shouted Karl. 'Sing a different song.'

'I only got one song,' Per snapped, 'and it's called the Truth.'

He spat onto the shingle.

'You got to listen to me, all of you, because this ain't a time for drinking or partying or using up precious food when we're already short and we got winter coming on. Have I got to spell it out to you? I shouldn't have to.'

He glared at them.

'We're ninety-seven people scratching an existence on a piece of rock at the back end of an archipelago. That's who we are. Get it into your bony heads. And get this too—nobody gives a damn about us. We're so far from the other islands they've practically stopped trading with us and the mainland might as well be in outer space. So we got to look out for ourselves like we always done, like our ancestors always done. Only now it's going to be more difficult than ever.'

'Why?' said Mungo from the front of the crowd.

'I'll tell you why, young man,' said Per.

12

He looked Mungo over, then peered once more into the group; and this time Hetty knew he was looking at her.

'I've had the same dream three nights in a row,' said Per, 'and this is the first time I've talked about it. But I got to tell you about it now because it's serious and it's true. There's evil coming to Mora—and it's already on its way.'

Hetty felt Tam lean close.

'Is that what you saw in your sea glass?' he whispered. 'Evil coming to Mora?'

She thought of the picture again and said nothing. Tam touched her on the arm.

'He's looking at you, Hetty.'

'I know, Tam,' she said.

And she turned and ran away down the beach.

# Chapter 3

She raced up the path to the top of the cliff and cut left towards Moon Cottage, Per's words pounding in her head.

'No,' she snarled back.

*There's evil coming to Mora.*

'No.'

*It's already on its way.*

'No, no, no.'

She reached Moon Cottage and stopped outside the door, breathing hard. All was dark around her. She thought of the old man, no doubt still fuming at his accusers, and perhaps even at her: he would certainly have seen her running away from the crowd. She listened for the sound of voices from the shingle beach below, but all she heard was the sea whispering up at her.

'What are you trying to tell me, ghost water?' she said.

No answer came. She stepped inside the cottage, closed the door behind her, and leaned back against it, drawing in the darkness of the room and the familiar smell of peat from the fire. The whispers faded into nothing and silence fell. She walked into the centre of the room and stopped again, locked in the stillness of the island.

There was something ageless about it, she decided, as though the present century had ceased to exist and she were living in some ancient time—and for a moment she almost felt it could be so. She didn't suppose the scents and sounds of Mora had ever changed much. But it wasn't just Mora that seemed ageless. She herself felt ageless too: as old and rootless as the wind. She heard Per's voice again, snapping in her head.

*There's evil coming to Mora.*

*It's already on its way.*

She pulled the sea glass from her pocket. It seemed as small and fragile as when she'd first found it on the shingle beach. She walked through to her bedroom, sat down at the little table, and lit a candle, then she searched for the image she had seen before: nothing at all, not even the hint of a picture, or a feeling that the object was worth coaxing. She gave it a few more minutes, then put it down, reached into the basket and took another piece of sea glass, her favourite blue and a friend of many years.

Nothing.

She tried another fragment from the basket, this one from Skull Cove, washed up last year. It too refused to speak. She moved the sea glass in front of the candle, watching the image of the flame beyond: a beautiful dancing form, but nothing unusual. She placed the sea glass on the desk, then picked up the first piece again.

'You gave me the image before,' she said to it. 'Why won't you give it to me again?'

But she spoke without any real hope. The glass was slim and dark and sensuous, but she'd been disappointed so many times. Indeed, when she'd had any success, it had often been with the nondescript pieces, the ones that seemed hardly worth collecting; and there was the other frustrating thing: one piece might work once, and then never work again.

This could be one such. She held the sea glass to the candle flame again and waited. Still nothing, just the flickering light beyond the glass, pressing towards her like fingers of flame. She eased her face closer, keeping the glass still. From the candle came a whisper of warmth.

'Show me your secret from the ghost water,' she said.

A ruffling of the glass, the smooth surface darkening. She watched, holding her breath. More darkness, tempered by the flame fighting for its place within her gaze, then a misty form.

'Who are you?' she whispered.

The image hung there, locked inside the glass. She watched, trembling, but there was no further change. She heard a spatter of rain against the window and stood up. On the far horizon she could see a distant glow. The rain grew heavier for a few moments, then eased to a drizzle. She held the sea glass against the windowpane. The image was still there, a small dark form caught in the glass, the liquid sky merging from behind; and she was sure now that it was the face she had seen before.

'You should be sleeping,' said Grandy behind her.

She looked round and saw her grandmother shaking her head.

'And you shouldn't be staring at those pieces of sea glass.'

'They're beautiful, Grandy.'

'I know they are,' said Grandy, 'and if that's all there was to it, I'd be happy. But you know exactly what I'm talking about.'

'I don't want to have this conversation again.'

'Come and sit by the fire,' said Grandy.

Hetty held the piece up in front of her.

'Look,' she said. 'Even you must see it this time.'

'I won't see it this time,' said Grandy, 'like I don't see it any time, and nobody else does either. Because there's nothing there.'

Hetty pushed the glass closer to Grandy's face.

16

'It's darker in the middle, see? It wasn't like that before. It got darker as I watched it, and now it's the shape of—'

'No, it isn't.' Grandy took the sea glass from her, peered at it for a moment, then handed it back. 'It's a piece of glass, Hetty. That's all it is, all it ever was. It's part of an old bottle that got dropped overboard from a ship or flung from a beach, and now the sea's smoothed it and given it to us as a lovely present to enjoy. But it's nothing more than that. It doesn't show pictures of the other world, however much you want it to.'

Grandy gave a sigh.

'Breaks my heart to see you fooling yourself like this. You're fifteen, you're a young woman, and the faces you're looking for disappeared when you were barely one year old. Your mother and father have moved on, Hetty, and you must do the same. You won't find their faces in a piece of sea glass. Or anybody else's. Now come and sit with me by the fire.'

Hetty pushed the sea glass into her pocket and followed her grandmother through to the main room.

'I notice you didn't touch any of the food at the party,' said Grandy.

Hetty didn't answer.

'I'm tired of telling you,' said Grandy. 'You never eat, never enough anyway. No wonder you're a waif of a thing. You know the first thing your mother and father will say to me when I meet them in the afterlife? Why didn't you feed her better?'

'And what will you say back?'

'I haven't thought that far ahead,' said Grandy. 'But let me get you something to eat now.'

'I don't want anything.'

'Hetty—'

'I don't want anything.' Hetty sat down by the fire and looked up. 'Please, Grandy. I don't want anything.'

Grandy watched her gravely for a while, then sat down next to her. More rain spattered the window.

'Is Per still talking doom and gloom?' said Hetty.

'He was when I left,' said Grandy, 'but I don't suppose he's got much of an audience now it's started to rain. And people were breaking up anyway. Except for Mackie and Rory and Karl and some of the others who wanted to carry on arguing with him.' Grandy sniffed. 'Seems a bit pointless to me.'

'They've got a good reason for wanting an argument with him.'

'And what would that be?'

'You know as well as I do,' said Hetty. 'Their fathers worked every bit as hard as Per and his cronies did to build *The Pride*. You've always told me they did.'

'That's true,' said Grandy, 'Mackie's father especially.'

'And now they're all dead and they can't defend themselves when Per makes out he did most of it himself. So Mackie and the others have to put him right.'

'I'm still not sure it's worth an argument with a tetchy old man on his hundredth birthday.'

'He's not just tetchy,' said Hetty. 'He's off his head.'

'That's probably why you dislike each other so much,' said Grandy.

'What's that supposed to mean?'

'You're too similar.'

'Grandy!'

'He's crazy and you're crazy.'

'Who says I'm crazy?'

Grandy laughed.

'You did. "I'm the only crazy person on Mora." That's what Tam told me you said to him up on the cliff-top.'

'He wasn't supposed to pass that on.'

Grandy laughed again.

'I'm only joking.'

'No, you're not,' said Hetty. 'You're serious.'

Grandy reached out and took her by the hand.

'You're not like Per,' she said. 'All right?'

Hetty looked away.

'I didn't like what he said this time,' she muttered.

'About building *The Pride*?'

'About evil coming to Mora.'

'That's just Per talking his usual rubbish,' said Grandy. 'Nothing to get bothered about.'

Hetty felt the sea glass again in her pocket.

'This is different,' she said.

'In what way?'

'He was staring at me when he talked about evil.'

'That's silly,' said Grandy. 'It was too dark to see which way his eyes were pointing.'

'He was looking at me, Grandy, and Tam thinks so too. He said so.'

She pictured the old man's face peering towards her over the heads of the others, his features fixed and angry; and then she pictured that other face, the one inside the sea glass: not fixed or angry, just . . . elusive. The rain grew heavier, drumming on the roof of Moon Cottage, then it eased once again. Hetty stood up.

'I'm going to bed, Grandy.'

'There's nothing to be frightened of, girl.'

'I didn't say I was frightened.'

'No, you didn't.'

They looked at each other for a moment, then Grandy reached out a hand.

'Give me a hug, sweetheart.'

Hetty leaned down and hugged her.

'And a kiss,' said Grandy.

Hetty kissed her. Grandy patted her on the back.

'Sleep well now,' she said, 'and if you find you can't, then come into my room and curl up with me.'

'All right,' said Hetty.

She walked through to the bathroom, washed herself, then made her way back to her own room and changed into her night clothes. The island was quiet again now. She let the stillness settle around her, then blew out the candle and climbed into bed. A few minutes later she heard Grandy doing the same next door. She lay back and listened, and it wasn't long before she caught the low, rhythmic snoring—a sound that had reassured her all her life. She closed her eyes and tried to sleep too. But sleep did not come.

What came was the storm.

# Chapter 4

She sensed it in the small hours: the whispers creeping from the silence, then rougher voices griping in
the deep and a vagrant moan of wind; the crash of
surf too, the first such sound for many weeks, and the
rain back again, heavier than before. Grandy came hurrying in, her wet-weather coat pulled over her night
clothes.

'None of us saw this coming,' she grumbled.

'Per'll say he did.'

Grandy grunted.

'Wait here.'

'I'll come with you.'

'No, stay inside. Not worth both of us getting wet.'

Grandy disappeared and a moment later Hetty saw her
through the window, checking all was secure outside. The
sounds of wind and surf grew louder. Hetty stared beyond the cliff. Sea and sky were both still dark but the sea
was shot through with streaks of white and it moved with
frightening intensity.

She changed into her day clothes, pulled on her coat
and boots, and ran outside. Lights were visible in the
cottages nearby and she could see figures checking hen
coops, lashing loose objects or carrying them indoors.
Grandy appeared round the side of the building.

'I told you to stay inside,' she said.

'I wanted to help.'

'No need. Everything's snug. All we can do now is keep warm and dry.'

Dawn revealed a tossing sea with angry waves driving upon the island. Tam arrived, his coat gleaming from the rain.

'You shouldn't be out in this,' said Grandy.

'I came to check you're both all right.'

'Why wouldn't we be?'

'I don't know,' said Tam. 'I just thought . . . '

Grandy chuckled.

'Get your coat off and have a hot drink. Hetty'll make it for you.'

'I can't, Grandy,' he said. 'I promised I'd get back in case Mother needed any help.'

'What's your father doing?'

'Going round the cottages,' said Tam, 'making sure everyone's all right. He's just been down to check *The Pride*. He went with Rory and the crew. They rowed out to make sure she's snug.'

'And is she?'

'She's fine,' said Tam. 'They're going to check her again later. Father said the sea's really rough outside the bay but the anchorage is calm as you like. Just as well we've got Eel Point.' He looked at Hetty. 'I went down too but they wouldn't let me row out with them to *The Pride* so I checked all the dinghies at the top of the beach. Yours is fine.'

'Thanks,' said Hetty.

'I pulled her a bit further up the shingle.'

'You didn't need to,' said Hetty. 'She was quite safe where she was.'

'That was good of you, Tam,' said Grandy.

She threw a glance at Hetty. Tam shrugged.

'Funny how this storm came out of nowhere,' he said. 'Maybe Per was on to something last night. What he said about trouble coming.'

'He didn't say trouble,' said Hetty. 'He said evil.'

'Whatever he said,' Grandy put in, 'it's nothing for anyone to worry about.'

'That's what Mother thinks,' said Tam. 'She also reckons this'll blow itself out by the end of the day.'

But the storm only grew worse. By late afternoon it was hammering the island with unrelenting malevolence. Hetty sat on her bed, staring at the sea glass, the image of the face still there: a strangely static thing against the turbulence outside. There was a heavier tone to the wind now and the ocean was a graveyard of torn rollers.

'Come and eat, Hetty,' said Grandy.

'I'm not hungry, Grandy,' she said.

The storm went on, through the night and into the next day, and on into another night, the air now filled with rain and blown spray and sounds so strident it felt to Hetty as though Mora herself were in pain. On the third day, the rain stopped but the wind increased to a terrifying new register. Hetty stood next to Grandy at the window and stared out.

'I've never known a storm like this,' said Grandy, 'even the one that took away your parents.'

'Grandy?'

'Yes, sweetheart.'

'Something terrible's going to happen. I just know it.'

Grandy frowned, then turned to the door and pulled on her coat and boots.

'I'm going out,' she said, 'just to see if I'm needed for anything. You stay here.'

Hetty waited till she'd gone, then pulled on her own heavy clothes and ran out of the cottage. She could feel the danger drawing close and could sense now what its target was. She tore down to Wolfstone Ridge, scrambled to the top of High Crag and sat down to steady herself

23

against the gale. Below her, the seas were mountainous as the wind hefted them towards the shore.

It wasn't one of these that destroyed *The Pride of Mora*. It was the collective ferocity of all of them, each wave building on the one before and growing in power and spite, as a force beyond Hetty's imagining exploded upon the island. She stared down in horror, the wind roaring about her. She knew the boat could not survive, yet even as she watched, she hoped for a miracle.

The boulders of Eel Point had never been breached in anyone's lifetime here, not even Per's, so there had to be a chance that the anchorage would remain safe and *The Pride of Mora* would ride her moorings as serenely as she had done through all previous storms. But in her heart Hetty knew this was different. A freak high tide was pushing the water steadily up the boulders of Eel Point. An hour later it broke over the top and waves drove upon the moored boat.

'Hetty!'

The cry reached her from below. She crawled back from the edge and searched the upper slopes of High Crag. Grandy was struggling up the path towards the summit.

'Go back, Grandy!' she called. 'Too windy up here!'

Grandy ignored her and clambered on. Hetty crawled back to her vantage point and stared down into the bay again. The situation was even worse than she'd feared. She'd expected *The Pride of Mora* to founder at her moorings and at least have some chance of being salvaged later, but the waves had ripped the hull clear and were forcing it onto the jagged rocks that straddled the shallow water close to the shingle beach. She saw Mackie leading Rory, Karl, and a group of other men into the surf. Grandy reached the summit, crawled out to join her and sat down, breathing heavily.

24

'Thought you'd be up here,' she said, 'but you shouldn't be. It's too risky, even sitting down.'

Hetty said nothing. Grandy took her arm and leaned against her, watching the men below.

'They're mad,' she said. 'It's too dangerous for that.'

*The Pride of Mora* was stuck on the rocks now, already dismasted. Eel Point was practically submerged and an unbroken procession of rollers was churning towards the stricken boat. Mackie and the men were in the thick of the surf, trying to wade or swim close enough to attach ropes to any parts of the boat they could reach, but it was no good: the seas were forcing them back. Mackie fell suddenly and disappeared under a comber.

Hetty gasped, but he soon reappeared, signalling to the other men. They closed round, fastened a safety rope to his waist, then took the end back to the beach and braced themselves. Mackie waded towards the boat again, coils of rope round his shoulder.

'This is foolish,' said Grandy. 'He'll get himself killed for nothing.'

Mackie went down again, felled by a huge wave. It was some moments before he rose, floundering, to the surface.

'He needs to get out of there,' said Grandy.

The boat started to roll. More waves broke upon the hull, the spray soaring high, but the men on the shore were pulling hard and, to Hetty's relief, they dragged Mackie clear. A moment later the cabin housing and some of the heavy tackle slid over the side and crashed into the space where he had been. He staggered back to the beach and joined the others.

'There's nothing they can do,' said Grandy.

The men seemed to have decided that too. They drew back to the top of the beach where the dinghies had been pulled to safety, and stood there, shivering, to watch the death of the island boat. As darkness fell, the hull started to break up. The moon rose amid chasing clouds to fling an impassive light upon the scene. The sides of the bay and the shingle beach were now lined with people collecting what wreckage they could.

Hetty stayed on the top of High Crag, crying softly.

'Come on, girl,' said Grandy. 'Let's go down.'

# *Chapter 5*

She let Grandy lead her down the slope and on to the path that descended to the bay. A cold rain started, sending a ghostly shadow upon the sea. Below them lights were showing in some of the cottages, and the moon revealed figures still moving about the bay and the shingle beach. On the quay they found Mackie coiling rope. He saw them and hurried over.

'Either of you seen Tam?' he said.

They shook their heads. Mackie looked anxiously about him.

'He's gone missing again—and what a time to do it. I told him not to wander off. Isla's gone looking for him and I'm about to do the same.'

'He's probably with Mungo,' said Hetty.

'He's not,' said Mackie. 'Mungo's down on the beach.'

Hetty scanned the shore and saw a group at the far end pulling flotsam from the surf. It was hard to make them all out in the darkness and the drizzle, but she could see Mungo and Duffy, and some of the boys from North Point. Nessa and Jinty were the only girls there, and there was no sign of Tam. She looked back at Mackie.

'Tam'll be all right. He knows how to look after himself.'

'He takes too many risks,' said Mackie, 'and so do you, Hetty. I saw you up on High Crag. You could have got blown off. You kids don't know how dangerous this wind is. Look at Mungo and the others. That surf's vicious and they're in and out of it like it's a millpond.'

'They're no more stupid than you were,' said Grandy, 'wading in up to your neck.'

But Mackie wasn't listening. He was staring round again, searching the darkness. Hetty reached into her pocket and touched the sea glass. It felt strangely comforting. Below her the waves went on pounding what was left of the hull. From behind came an unwelcome voice.

'I did try to warn everybody.'

She groaned and looked round. Old Per was standing on the quay with Gregor, Harold, and Lorna, and some of his other friends. He watched her for a moment, then turned and spat to the side.

'But nobody took a blind bit of notice. Like they never does.'

Hetty looked away.

'Anybody listening?' said Per. 'Or am I talking to myself as usual?'

'Have you seen Tam?' said Mackie.

'No, I ain't,' said the old man, and then, 'What's up with Hetty?'

'Leave Hetty alone,' said Grandy.

'I said what's up with Hetty?'

Hetty stared out into the bay and said nothing.

'I'm talking to you, girl,' spluttered the old man, 'only you ain't listening again, are you? Like you wasn't listening last night on the beach. I saw you running away, and I know why. You're so bunged up with your sea glass nonsense you don't like the proper truth when you hear it.'

Hetty started to walk towards the landing stage.

'Hetty!' called Grandy. 'Come back!'

Hetty carried on walking. A moment later she heard footsteps behind her, then Mackie caught her by the arm.

'No further, Hetty. Look down there.'

'I know.'

She'd already seen the waves breaking over the end of the landing stage. She kept her eyes on the left-hand arc of the bay, where the outermost rocks were drowning in foam. The moon had brightened them and, with the rain now easing again, they had a chilly luminosity.

'There,' she said, pointing.

'What's to see?' said Mackie.

She looked round at him.

'Tam. He's on the top of Crab Rock.'

'He's what!'

She turned and looked again. Tam had not only managed to climb the great rock but he had even crawled out along its curved tip, the waves crashing against the base below him, and he was now gazing over the sea. Mackie gave a roar.

'The stupid little—'

'Wait,' said Hetty. 'There's something else.'

'I don't care. I'm getting that boy back here.'

'Mackie!'

But he was already pulling her towards the quay.

'Mackie!'

She wrenched her arm free.

'Hetty, this is stupid,' he said. 'I've got to get to Tam and—'

'He's not there, Mackie.'

'He's what?'

'He's not there. Look.'

She pointed to Crab Rock. There was no one on top now.

'Oh, God,' said Mackie.

'It's all right,' she said quickly. 'He's climbed down. He's running back to the shore.'

Mackie stared.

'You're right,' he said. 'I can see him.'

'But there's something else,' she said. 'It's what I saw before. It might be what Tam was looking at. Why he climbed Crab Rock.'

'What do you mean?'

Grandy joined them, panting.

'What's happening?' she said.

Hetty stared over the water, the sea glass tight in her hand.

'I'm sure I saw a boat.'

She searched again for the moving shape. She'd only seen it once, bobbing on a wave crest before disappearing into a trough.

'There!'

A small craft, no bigger than a rowing boat. There was no sign of anyone in it. She heard a shout from the side of the bay. It was Tam's voice.

'There's a boat!'

She peered round and saw him standing on the path that cut back to the quay round the base of the cliff. He gestured towards Crab Rock.

'Beyond the point!' he yelled.

She turned and looked again. The boat was still visible, and now Mackie had seen it too.

'It's heading for the rocks,' he said. 'Come on.'

They hurried back to the quay where a crowd was now forming as people ran up from the beach or down from the higher ground. Mungo and the others were there too but the eyes of all were fixed on the point. There was no mistaking the boat now as it surfed towards the rocks.

'Is there anyone in it?' said Mackie.

'Hard to tell,' said Grandy.

Tam arrived, breathlessly.

'Can you see it?'

'Never mind,' said Mackie. 'Go find your mother. She's worried sick about you. We'll talk later.' He turned to some of the men standing by. 'I'm heading for the point. That boat's going to hit any moment and there might be someone on board. Karl? Rory? Come with me?'

Both nodded.

'Don't go near that boat,' said Per.

Mackie threw a baleful look at him.

'And why not?'

'It's part of the evil,' he muttered. 'I saw it in my dream.'

'It's not evil,' said Hetty.

The old man glowered at her.

'What do you know about it?'

She felt the sea glass again, unsure why she'd spoken.

'I just know it's not,' she said.

'It's evil!' he screamed. 'Everything about it's evil!'

The boat crashed on the outermost rock. Hetty watched, aware of Mackie and the men running towards the point, and Tam stepping close. Somehow the boat was still afloat—another wave had lifted it clear of the first rock and was driving it further inshore. It bumped against the base of Crab Rock and skewed round, then tipped momentarily to starboard. As it did so, she saw a figure crouching in the bottom.

'There's someone in the boat!' she shouted.

But already the glimpse was gone. Another wave had driven the boat round the point and out of view. She tried to picture the figure. There had been no sense of a face, just a dark form. Talk burst out all around her.

'We should help Mackie,' someone said.

There was a roar of agreement and the crowd started to disperse, most people setting off towards the point. Hetty felt Tam take her by the arm.

'Hetty,' he said, 'let's watch from higher up.'

Grandy glanced at him.

'You should be looking for Isla. Like your father told you to.'

'I will,' he said, 'but I want to see what happens. Can Hetty come with me?'

'Hetty?' said Grandy. 'Do you want to?'

But Hetty was still picturing the figure in the boat. She stroked the sea glass, thinking hard, then realized they were both watching her.

'I'll go with Tam,' she said.

'All right,' said Grandy, 'but be careful on the high places. This wind's lethal. I'll have some soup ready for you when you get back to the cottage. If I'm not there, it means I'm helping the others, so start without me.'

And Grandy turned away.

'Let's go,' said Tam.

# *Chapter 6*

They raced up as far as Broken Tooth Ridge, then stopped and stared back down. Even in the darkness Hetty could see the wreckage from *The Pride of Mora* washing about the bay, the waves still thundering past Eel Point and onto the shingle beach, and over to the left, the white water frothing around Crab Rock. Figures were moving there already, most of them on the safe ground closer to the cliff, but Mackie, Karl, and Rory were clambering over the jagged rocks where Tam had been earlier. There was no sign of the small boat.

'It's been driven up the coast,' said Tam. 'Come on. If we cut past Gregor's place, we might be able to see it.'

And he ran on up the slope. Hetty followed, her mind on Per's words down at the quay, and on her own back to him: she still wasn't sure why she'd said what she'd said.

'Come on, Hetty,' called Tam.

He was waiting for her at the top of the cliff. She caught him up and they ran together to Holm Edge. She stayed well back, frightened of the gusts, but Tam dropped onto all fours and crawled to the brink, the wind whipping his hair and clothes.

'Tam,' she called, 'don't go so far.'

He glanced round at her.

'It's all right.'

'You're too close to the edge.'

'I just want to see over.'

33

She stayed where she was and stared at the sea. It was like a vast, snapping jaw. Tam peered down for a while, then pulled back and joined her again.

'I couldn't see the boat,' he said. 'Let's try further up.'

'We should be looking for your mother.'

'She'll be fine.'

He ran on down the track towards Skull Cove. Hetty followed again, aware of a growing tension inside her. Gregor's land opened to the left, his sheep and goats moving about the grass, his cottage dark.

'There!' called Tam.

He had stopped just ahead and was pointing down into Skull Cove. Hetty ran up and joined him.

'See?' he said. 'Down there.'

She could just make out the boat thumping against the boulders where the arm of the cove braced itself against the sea. They scrambled off the track and down to the stony base of Skull Cove. The boat was breaking up fast. Even in the few minutes it had taken them to climb down, the hull had split in several places, some of the sections floating onto the smaller rocks, others drifting free. Tam ignored the surf and splashed straight into the shallows. Hetty called after him.

'Be careful, Tam!'

'It's fine,' he yelled. 'It's not like the bay.'

She studied the shore. Tam was right in that the surf was less violent here, being partially blocked by the rocky bar at the southern end of the cove, but it was still rough, and the waves further out, where there was no land to check them, looked as hostile as any she had seen from High Crag. She looked back at Tam. He was now wading towards the nearest pieces of wreckage. She hurried along the shore, anxious that he'd do something foolhardy in an attempt to reach them, but he stopped at last, waist-deep in the water, and looked round at her.

'It's not dangerous, Hetty.'

'It was dangerous climbing on Crab Rock.'

He shrugged.

'I saw this speck out at sea, and everybody else was busy with *The Pride*, so I climbed Crab Rock to get a better view and spotted the boat. Maybe it was a bit of a risk. But it's not dangerous here. I just wanted to get a closer look at that stuff floating over there. I thought it was a body for a moment, but it's just the thwart.'

He waded back to the shore and stood beside her, dripping.

'Can you see anyone in the water?' he said.

'No.'

She stared into the darkness. The cove looked eerie in the night and the desolate destruction of this tiny boat made it somehow feel more so. Again she pictured the figure crouched in the bottom. It was hard to believe anyone could survive a storm like this in such a small craft. She squeezed the sea glass again and frowned.

'Did you get a clear view of the person in the boat, Tam?'

'No,' he said, 'and I don't suppose I will now. The body's probably been washed out to sea.'

'Not necessarily.'

'What do you mean?'

She pointed over the water.

'Some of those rocks are flat and low,' she said. 'If the boat struck in the right place, you could scramble onto one of them and pick your way to the shore.'

She turned and stared around Skull Cove. There was no sign of anyone on the slopes, but the darkness made it hard to see. Then she saw figures moving on the high ground. A moment later there was a shout.

'Tam!'

It was Mungo, with Duffy, Nessa, and Jinty behind him. They started down the slope, the boys scrambling on ahead. Mungo arrived first.

'You'd better brace yourself,' he said to Tam. 'Your mother's on the way.'

The others arrived, crowding round. Jinty stared towards the rocks.

'You've found the boat,' she said.

She ran down to the water's edge, followed by Nessa. From the top of the cove came another shout.

'Tam!'

It was Isla this time. A moment later Mackie appeared too, with some of the men from the bay. Tam looked at Hetty.

'Come with me, can you?'

'All right.'

'We'll come too,' said Mungo.

'I just want Hetty,' said Tam.

Mungo looked at her, then at Tam.

'Suit yourself,' he said.

Tam took his time climbing to the top of the slope, but it only made Isla more angry.

'What the hell do you think you're doing?' she snapped. She grabbed him by the arm and cuffed him round the head. 'Up and down the island I've been—'

'Mother—'

'Up and down like a demented fool, looking for you, worrying myself sick, and where were you? On the top of Crab Rock!'

She cuffed him again.

'Isla,' said Hetty, 'Tam's found the boat.'

36

'I don't care what he's done,' said Isla. 'He's still—'

'Hold on,' said Mackie. He looked at Tam. 'You found the boat?'

Tam pointed to the rocks.

'Down there,' he said. 'It's broken up but you can still see some of the bits floating about.'

'Did you spot anyone in the water?'

'No,' said Tam, 'but Hetty thinks you could maybe get ashore by climbing over those rocks.'

Mackie stared at them for a moment, then turned to the men.

'Possible, I suppose?'

Rory shook his head. So did most of the others.

'More likely they drowned, Mackie,' said Karl.

'Maybe,' said Mackie, 'but Hetty could be right. We'd better go on looking just in case.' He ran his eye over Mungo, Duffy, and the girls who had now climbed back up to the track. 'You kids should be at your homes, not running about in this storm.'

'We could help with the search,' said Nessa.

'All right,' said Mackie, 'but you're to work in pairs, understood? I don't want people searching on their own.'

But half an hour later, no one had found anything. Mackie walked over to where Hetty and Tam were clambering among the rocks on the southern slope.

'Enough now,' he said. 'Tam, your mother's going home and you're to go with her. No arguments. She's waiting for you up the top there.'

'All right, Father.'

Tam glanced at Hetty, then set off up the slope.

'Good boy,' said Mackie. 'Hetty?'

'I know.'

'Back to Moon Cottage,' he said, 'and if Grandy's not there, you're to wait for her. No more rushing about the island in the dark. Do you want me to walk with you? Mungo and the others seem to have cleared off.'

'I'm all right.'

'Off you go, then, girl. Be careful going past Holm Edge.'

'What are you and the men going to do?'

'Carry on with the search,' said Mackie.

She saw Karl, Rory, and the others waiting for him on the path at the northern end of the cove. She climbed to the top and ran back towards Holm Edge. Below her the sea looked wilder than ever. The gusts, too, seemed to be increasing. She stepped from the shelter of the hill, steadied herself, then hurried past Holm Edge and down the track that led to the bay. It opened before her like a foaming mouth, Eel Point white with spray, Crab Rock glowing in the night. She stopped at Broken Tooth Ridge and stared down.

Nothing remained of *The Pride of Mora*.

# *Chapter 7*

Moon Cottage was deserted. Hetty walked round to make sure Grandy wasn't asleep in bed or busy at her spinning wheel, then she returned to the main room and stepped over to the window. The sea below seemed to snarl up at her. She thought of the figure in the boat, then pulled the sea glass from her pocket and held it against the pane: the face was still there, dark but clear. An hour later she was still staring at it. The door opened and Grandy trudged in.

'I'm only staying for a bit, Hetty,' she said.

Hetty thrust the sea glass back in her pocket.

'Where have you been?'

'Helping Anna and Dolly in the chapel,' said Grandy. 'Mackie's asked people to report any news to them and he's keeping in touch by sending runners. I said I'd go back again after I've checked you're all right and drunk a bit of soup. Have you saved me any?'

'All of it.'

'You haven't had any yourself?' Grandy shook her head. 'I don't know why I bother.'

Hetty helped her off with her boots.

'I don't want another lecture, Grandy,' she said.

Grandy lifted the lid from the cooking pot hanging over the fire.

'Smells delicious,' she said. 'I don't know how you could resist it.'

Hetty fetched the big mugs, Grandy ladled soup into each one, and they sat down by the fire.

'Go on, then,' said Grandy.

Hetty took a sip.

'It's good,' she said.

'I know it is,' said Grandy. 'That's why I wanted you to get some inside you. Especially on a night like this.'

They drank in silence for a few minutes, the wind still pounding the cottage.

'Poor old building's going to blow away one day,' said Grandy.

'It's been here two hundred years, you keep telling me.'

'Well, it won't be here another two hundred.'

Grandy drained her mug and stood up.

'Want some more?'

'I haven't finished mine.'

Grandy peered over the top of Hetty's mug.

'You're not even halfway through it, girl. Go on, drink.'

Hetty took another sip.

'That's not drinking,' said Grandy. 'Do it properly. I'll watch it go down.'

Hetty struggled through the rest of the soup.

'Don't tell me you didn't like it,' said Grandy.

'I did,' said Hetty. 'It's good. I told you.'

'Want some more?'

'No, thanks.'

'Sure?'

'I don't want any. Please, Grandy.'

'Give me your mug.'

Grandy placed both mugs on the floor and leaned back in the chair.

'I hear you and Tam found the boat smashed up in Skull Cove.'

'Who told you?'

'Mackie. I saw him with some of the men from the search party.'

'So they haven't found anybody?'

'No,' said Grandy, 'and I don't suppose they will. Whoever was in that boat's probably drowned by now. I don't believe for one moment they made it to the shore, whatever anyone else says. So that's another death in Mora's waters, and God knows when we're going to be able to report it, now we haven't got a seagoing boat any more.'

'I still can't believe we've lost *The Pride*,' said Hetty.

'Neither can I,' said Grandy. 'She was such a fine vessel I thought she'd go on for ever. I think we all did. It was hard to watch her break up on the rocks when I can still picture her being built all those years ago.'

'Do you remember it really clearly?'

'Oh, yes,' said Grandy. 'Dolly and I used to take the men their food every day. We saw every stage of the building and I can see the men in my mind clear as I'm seeing you now. Hard workers, all of them, and some big characters among them, mostly all dead now, of course. But Mackie's father held them together. He was the one they listened to.'

'I knew it wasn't Per,' said Hetty.

'Per was part of it though,' said Grandy. 'So was Gregor, so was Harold, and they worked as hard as everybody else. They've every right to be proud of what they did.'

'They're proud all right,' said Hetty.

Grandy poked the fire, then turned to look at her again.

'You're very hard sometimes, Hetty,' she said.

'What do you mean?'

'You've got to make space for people you don't like, you know.'

'I can't make space for Per.'

'Hetty—'

'I'll never make space for Per,' she said. 'He's horrible to me over the sea glass and he's horrible to anyone else he doesn't like. He's puffed up and superstitious and he thinks just because he's the oldest person on the island we've all got to listen to him.'

'You don't have to listen to him.'

'Some people do.'

'And some people don't,' said Grandy. 'I agree he's a difficult old man. But remember this—he lost a son in the storm that took your parents, as you well know.'

'Dolly lost a husband, but she's not twisted like Per.'

'We all react differently to these things,' said Grandy. 'Look around you. There's scarcely a family on Mora hasn't lost someone to the sea down the generations, and some families have lost many. Per's line will end when he dies. So don't be hard on him.'

Hetty shrugged.

'He was miserable before his son died. Everyone says so. You've said so.'

'Yes,' said Grandy, 'but you're still being unfair on him. Per's lived a very long life, remember. He's seen a lot of people drown, many of them like your mother and father, and Dolly's husband, and his own son, putting off in rowing boats to try to rescue someone else, and never coming back. It's hard to see so much tragedy without becoming bitter or fatalistic. That's why I want you to be strong, Hetty.'

'You saying I'm weak?'

'Of course not,' said Grandy. 'You could never be weak, coming from parents like yours. But . . . '

'But what?' said Hetty.

Grandy took her hand and squeezed it.

'Hetty, do you know what the people of Mora depend on most to stay alive?'

Hetty didn't answer.

'Because it's not our animals or our crops or our fishing,' Grandy went on, 'or what we get from trading our wool and stone.'

'What is it, then?'

'We depend on our spirit,' said Grandy. 'Those other things too, of course, but most of all we depend on our spirit. That's the strength I'm talking about, Hetty. That's how we endure. That's how our ancestors endured. Because that's what it comes down to, sweetheart. If we don't endure, we don't survive.'

Hetty looked away.

'How will we survive without a boat, Grandy?'

'Mackie will organize a team and build another one. He's not his father's son for nothing. And Tam will be just like him. When he grows up a bit and stops taking silly risks. But we both know why he does that.'

'I don't.'

'I think you know it very well,' said Grandy. 'You're pretending you haven't noticed because it's unsettling you, and I can understand that. You and Tam have been best friends since you were born, but now he's looking at you in a different way and trying to impress you, like the other boys are.'

The fire crackled. The wind went on roaring outside.

'I don't want to talk about Tam,' said Hetty.

'All right.'

'And you're wrong about the other boys,' she said. 'They just think I'm mad.'

Grandy laughed.

'I'm old but I'm not blind,' she said. 'Mungo and Duffy might play the fool around you but get Duffy on his own and he's an open book to me. And it's not just him. Why have the Halvorson brothers started walking with you to

43

the schoolhouse in the mornings? It's not exactly on their way. And why do the boys from North Point keep turning up at the door? Do you think they tramp all the way from the top of the island just to see me?'

'Can we drop this, Grandy?'

A stronger gust thundered against the side of the cottage. Hetty hooked a hand inside her grandmother's arm and leaned against her.

'You're cold, Grandy,' she said.

'Warming up, girl.'

Hetty glanced at her. Grandy was still fearsomely resilient, like Dolly and Anna and most of the older women on the island, but in the last year there had been a change. For the first time ever her grandmother had seemed mortal. Grandy caught her look.

'Stop worrying, Hetty. I'm not going to die just yet.'

Shadows from the fire flickered over their bodies. Grandy stood up.

'I'd better get back to the chapel. If I stay here much longer, I'll nod off. If anyone turns up looking for me, tell them where I am.'

'I could come with you.'

'You can stay here and get some sleep,' said Grandy.

And with a warning glance, she shrugged on her coat and left.

Hetty looked over the fire, laid on more peat and watched the glow for a few minutes; then she made her way back to her room. But she didn't change into her night clothes. She was too keyed up for sleep. She climbed onto the bed and lay there, listening to the storm beating upon the cottage, her mind once again on the figure in the boat, and on the sea glass in her pocket. For some reason she felt unwilling to look at it again.

Somehow she dozed, in spite of her restlessness; then suddenly she woke again. The darkness was swirling, as though something had disturbed it. She sat up and peered about her, then climbed off the bed and walked through to the main room. The noise outside had changed. The crash of the sea and the howl of the wind had somehow commingled into a roar so vast she could no longer tell the individual sounds apart. She stopped in the middle of the room, frightened of the cacophony beyond the walls.

Then she heard a shout.

# Chapter 8

She stared towards the sea. She was certain the voice had come from that direction. But all she heard was the roar of the storm. She walked up to the window and peered out. Below her was a chaos of white water as wave after wave drove towards the island. Then something moved, closer to the cottage: a man, framed in the darkness. The shout came again.

'Hetty!'

And she recognized both the voice and the man.

'Crazy fool,' she murmured. 'Startling me like that.'

It was old Gregor. He shuffled up to the window, stared through at her for a few moments, then gestured towards the door of the cottage. She nodded and ran to open it. He was some moments arriving, and he didn't come in. He just stood there, wheezing.

'Didn't you hear me?' he said.

'I heard you shout.'

'Before that. I knocked on the door.'

'The storm's very loud,' she said. 'What do you want?'

'I'm looking for Grandy.' The old man glanced over his shoulder, then back at her. 'I seen a figure on the west side. Crawling, I thought, though I couldn't be sure.'

'The west side?'

Gregor nodded.

'Heading towards Scar Cliff, it was. I was some way off and couldn't see clear, but it ain't one of us, not moving like that. Didn't know if I ought to go and warn the others down that way or come and find someone quicker on their feet to do it. Moon Cottage is nearer so I came here. Thought Grandy could maybe send you. Is she here?'

'She's at the chapel helping Anna and Dolly.'

'Can you go and tell her?' said Gregor. 'They've probably got a runner there. And someone'll need to tell Mackie. You go ahead. I'll follow in my own time.'

Hetty pulled on her coat and boots and set off down the path. The wind drove her back at once. She dipped her body and staggered forward. The roar had now turned to an all-engulfing shriek. She stumbled on, keeping low, and eventually reached the track that twisted towards the centre of the island.

She forced herself down it, anxious to find some protection from the wind. The ridges on either side offered something of a shield, but even here the gale whirled about her. She pulled her coat more tightly around her and pressed on. The track bore right, then straightened again, and she saw at last the familiar outlines of the meeting hall, the schoolhouse, and Anna's cottage.

All were dark and, to her surprise, so was the chapel further down. A violent rain shower started. She ducked under the schoolhouse porch and waited for it to pass, then hurried on to the chapel, and this time noticed a light flickering round the edges of the door. She pushed it open and the light disappeared. From inside the chapel came Anna's voice.

'Come in quickly and I'll relight the candle.'

She closed the door behind her and stared towards the altar. Three cloudy figures were there, Grandy and Dolly sitting down, Anna on her feet. A moment later a match flared, and the candle burned once more. Anna turned towards her.

'We didn't expect to see you, Hetty.'

'I thought there was no one here,' she said. 'I didn't see the light at first.' She hesitated. 'Were you all praying?'

'Yes,' said Anna. 'It seemed the best thing to do while we were waiting for the next runner from Mackie. Have you got some news?'

'Yes.'

'Come and tell us.'

Hetty glanced at Grandy, then walked up to the altar. The shriek of the storm seemed strangely muted in the chapel.

'I'm sorry I made the light go out,' she said.

'It's only a candle, Hetty,' said Anna.

But now the new flame vanished too.

'Who's that?' said Dolly, peering towards the entrance.

'Gregor,' came the answer.

The old man stood there, swaying on his feet. His coat and hair were sodden. Dolly bustled over and took him by the arm.

'Come and sit down, Gregor.'

'I didn't mean to let the storm in,' he said.

He sat down, puffing hard, while Anna relit the candle.

'The rain started coming down heavy,' he said, 'so I ran. But I shouldn't have. Better to get soaked than have my heart banging away like this. Have you told them, Hetty?'

'I just got here.'

'How come you took so long?'

'I sheltered from the rain on the way.'

Gregor shook his head.

'You should have kept on running. No time to waste.'

'What's happened?' said Anna.

'I seen someone,' said Gregor. 'Wasn't clear who but it was someone creeping, I thought. Heading for Scar Cliff.

Wasn't nobody from Mora, I'm certain of that. Someone should warn the others down there and tell Mackie and his team. You got a runner here?'

'There's no one at the moment,' said Anna.

'Send Hetty, then.'

Grandy shook her head.

'I don't want Hetty going.'

'I can do it,' said Hetty.

'Someone's got to go,' said Gregor, 'and Hetty's quicker than you three put together. Long as she don't stop again to keep herself dry.'

Hetty opened her mouth to retort, then changed her mind.

'I can go,' she said quietly.

'She'll be all right, Grandy,' said Anna. 'She's fast and sensible.'

'Fast, yes.'

'Grandy!' said Hetty.

'All right,' said Grandy. She turned to Hetty. 'Find someone on that side of the island, tell them what Gregor's seen, then go back to Moon Cottage.'

'I'll find Mackie too.'

'No, Hetty, I don't want—'

But Hetty was gone. She ran towards the western bluff, the wind pummelling her face and body. Below her the sea was white against the rocks as the rollers hammered the shore. She stopped at Wolfstone Ridge and looked about her. Before her was the path to Scar Cliff and the cottages on this corner of the island. On an impulse she cut left and started to climb High Crag. She reached the top and braced herself against the squalls.

The waves looked more frightening than ever from up here, but she kept well back from the edge and turned to stare north. Mora lay below her, a mixture of dark and bright, depending on where the moon-glow fell. She could see the curvature of the land, the paths and tracks crisscrossing the ridges, the scattered cottages, the undulating ground towards the centre of the island, the outlines of the rocks and hillocks.

No sign of a crawling figure, or anybody at all. She scrambled down the slope again and rejoined the path that led to the cottages that hugged the rocky shoulder just in from Scar Cliff. Two minutes later she was outside the first. She stared at the door, clenching and unclenching her fists. She knew she should knock here first, but it was the one cottage on the island she had no wish to visit. She thought of Hal and Sara's place just a short sprint away. Perhaps she could give them the news and they could pass it on here. Then the door opened and she saw Per peering out at her. The old man had his wet-weather clothes and boots on, and a stick in his hand. He ran a scornful eye over her.

'Wasn't going to knock, was you?' he growled. 'Going to run straight past to one of the other cottages, one of the "nice" cottages, right? Hal and Sara's nice, you're thinking. I'll call on them. No need to bother with nasty, horrible, beastly old Per. Don't think I can't see it, girl.'

He looked her up and down.

'What's your news?'

'Gregor thinks he's seen a figure heading this way.'

'I was expecting this,' said Per. 'That's why I'm dressed ready.'

He stepped out of the cottage, closed the door, and stared into the darkness.

'The evil's abroad,' he said. 'It's on Mora now.'

'You don't know the figure's evil.'

He whirled round and faced her.

'Of course it's evil, you idiot of a girl.'

'Don't speak to me like that.'

'Did you think I just meant losing *The Pride* when I talked of evil down on the beach?' The old man glared at her. 'But of course you wasn't listening, was you? Because you never does. If you did listen, young lady, I might be able to push some of that sea glass nonsense out of your head.'

'And push some of your own nonsense in,' said Hetty.

She turned and set off down the path. The old man bellowed after her.

'Where do you think you're going?'

She stopped and turned round.

'To warn the others.'

'Wait there!'

Per hobbled up to her.

'I'll come too,' he grumbled. 'Make sure you don't tell 'em nothing stupid.'

'Long as we don't have to talk to each other on the way,' she said.

They tramped off together, fighting the gusts in the gaps between ridges. Over to the left, the sea boiled around the base of Scar Cliff. It took them some minutes to reach Sara and Hal's cottage.

'Light in the window,' said the old man.

Hetty had already noticed it. She'd also seen Sara peering out at them. A moment later the door opened and Hal beckoned them closer. They walked up to the door and saw Sara waiting there too.

'Sara's seen someone,' said Hal. 'A face at the window.'

'Did you get a clear view?' Per said to her.

Sara shook her head.

'Just a dark face with hair swirling, then it was gone.'

'How long ago?'

'Half an hour,' said Sara. 'I know I should have gone and warned people but I was frightened with Hal not being there.'

'I've only been back a couple of minutes,' said Hal. 'I've been on the east side with one of the search parties, and I was about to go out again to tell everyone about this figure.'

He glanced at his wife.

'Let's all go,' he said.

The four of them set off down the track, the wind rising again. Hetty said nothing. She was searching the ground about her. She felt sure she knew every hiding place on Mora, but for the first time in her life the island felt threatening. They reached the next cottage and saw Rab and Ailsa in the doorway.

'They know already,' said Sara.

Rab hurried out to join them.

'What's happened?' said Hal.

'Ailsa thinks she heard something.'

Hetty looked over at Ailsa, hanging back in the doorway.

'She all right?' said Hal.

'Bit scared,' said Rab. 'Says she heard a scream outside the cottage.'

'Did you hear it?'

'Not with this wind. But I don't doubt Ailsa did.'

They walked closer to the doorway and Ailsa dropped her eyes.

'Easy, Ailsa,' said Sara.

'Tell them what you heard,' said Rab.

'This scream,' said Ailsa. 'It was like . . . I don't know . . . '

She turned and disappeared inside the cottage.

'I'm sorry,' said Rab, 'but she won't say no more.'

Hetty saw Per watching her darkly.

'Believe me now, girl?' he muttered. 'About the evil abroad?'

'No, I don't believe you,' she said.

'Well, you should.'

Per scowled at the others.

'And so should all of you,' he added. 'Only none of you ever does.'

'Not now, old man,' said Hal. 'Rab, you stay with Ailsa. The rest of us'll check the other cottages and try to find Mackie.'

The remaining cottages on this limb of the island were clustered round the bend in the cliff. But there were no lights visible and nobody answered the doors.

'There!' said Hetty.

Figures were moving on the higher slopes.

'Come on,' said Hal.

But Per stepped in front of him.

'I ain't struggling up there just to talk to Mackie and his friends.'

'Then go back to your cottage,' said Hal.

'I will,' said the old man, and with a final glower, he set off into the darkness.

Hal turned to the others.

'Let's go.'

They climbed the path that twisted up from the cottages and scrambled on through the rocky outcrops. The search party was spread across the high ground among disparate flocks of sheep. Hetty spotted Mackie at once; but he was less certain of them.

'Who's there!' he roared.

'Only us, Mackie,' Hal called back.

They joined him near the top of the hill, the wind beating them savagely.

'Sorry,' said Mackie. 'Didn't see the rest of you, just saw Hal. And he looked strange in the darkness. Not that he looks better in daylight.'

A scream flew down on the wind.

'There it is again,' said Mackie.

'You've heard it before?' said Hal.

'Just a few minutes ago.'

'Rab says Ailsa heard it too.'

Hetty checked upwind, aware of the others doing the same, but she could see no one else on the slopes apart from the searching figures. She caught sight of Tam among them. He saw her at the same moment and came running over.

'I thought you were at home,' she said.

'Father said I could come out again and help. Stay with me for a bit?'

'All right.'

'Not for long,' said Mackie. 'Hetty needs her rest.'

'I'm fine,' she said quickly.

But it was no use. Weariness was catching up with her at last. She forced herself on, plodding next to Tam as the search party worked towards the north, but there were no further screams and no sightings of a strange figure. Tam caught her by the arm and stopped her.

'Go home, Hetty.'

'I'm all right.'

'You're not. You're exhausted.'

She looked at him, then managed a smile.

'Thanks, Tam,' she said. 'I'll see you.'

By the time she reached Moon Cottage she was aching with fatigue. There was no sign of Grandy. She tidied the fire, then wandered over to the window and stared out. A fractured moon was pushing through the clouds to brighten the horizon, but there was no hint of daylight.

She felt the sea glass in her pocket again, still wary of it, then made herself pull it out. The picture of the face was still there. She pushed the sea glass back in her pocket, but the image remained, clear in her mind. Rain started to fall again. She trudged to her room, slumped on the bed, and fell asleep in her clothes.

# Chapter 9

When she woke, it was well past dawn. The rain had stopped but the storm was still raging. She jumped off the bed and checked round the cottage. Grandy was not there, but the fire had been made up and some bread and cheese left on the table. She slipped on her coat and boots, and hurried out of the cottage.

A fragile sun was struggling up the sky. She looked about her, searching for someone who might give her news, but there was no one to be seen. She ran to High Crag and scrambled to the top. The island lay before her like an open palm. But Mora appeared to be deserted.

She stared down. It was almost as though she were the only person on the island, like the mythical hermit who was said to have lived here back in some distant age, though hardly anybody believed in him. Then she saw a figure running towards Wolfstone Ridge.

'Tam!' she yelled.

He looked up and beckoned furiously. She picked her way down as quickly as she could and met him at the bottom.

'I've been looking for you,' he said. 'Come on.'

He grabbed her hand and started to pull her after him.

'Wait,' she said. 'What's happened?'

He stopped, still holding her hand.

'I just met Mungo. He said Rory's search party's found someone.'

'Where?'

'Near Hermit's Grotto. That's all I know. Come on.'

And he tugged her again.

'Tam, let go, can you?'

He hesitated.

'I'm quicker on my own,' she said.

He let go and they raced down the track as far as the schoolhouse, then cut left up the middle of the island. Hetty looked about her as she ran. It was clear that others had already heard the news. The fields were empty and there were no sounds at all from the cottages. They crossed Horn Ridge and ran on through the peat land to North Point, the great cliffs falling away on either side and Hermit's Grotto down to the left.

'They're supposed to be somewhere round here,' said Tam, looking about him. 'Unless Mungo was making it all up.'

Hetty ran round the grotto to the path that led down the side of the cliff.

'Tam!' she called.

He hurried over to her.

'There,' she said, pointing down.

The stony beach by the north-western point was crowded with people, most of the community as far as she could tell, including Grandy, Mackie, and old Per. They were staring over the chain of rocks that curled from the shore out into the sea. At the end was a figure peering back at them: a small, ancient woman.

Hetty stiffened.

'It's her, Tam,' she said.

'Who?'

'The face I saw in the sea glass.'

'You mean the thing you wouldn't tell me about up on the cliff-top?'

Hetty went on staring at the woman. Even from this distance there was no mistaking the face. She felt in her pocket for the sea glass, touched it, and let go.

'I can't believe it, Tam,' she said. 'It's almost like . . . '
She frowned.

'Almost like she's come through all this just to find me.'

She hurried down the path, her eyes on the woman. It seemed inconceivable that someone so frail could have survived so much: the storm, the voyage in a small boat, the crash on the shore of Skull Cove, the night spent crawling over the island, and now these slippery rocks. How the woman had clambered to the end of them was a mystery. But Hetty had no doubts as to the reason why.

'We've got to stop her,' she murmured.

'Doing what?' said Tam, close to her shoulder.

'She wants to kill herself.'

'How do you know?'

'I just do. She's lost the will to go on.'

'But I thought you said she's come to find you.'

'She hasn't seen me yet.'

They ran onto the beach and pushed through the crowd. Nobody took any notice of them. The eyes of all were on the woman at the end of the rocks. She had now turned her back to them and was staring towards the waves thundering on the north-western point. Hetty felt her grandmother move alongside her.

'Wondered when you'd turn up,' said Grandy.

Hetty said nothing. She was still staring at the woman, willing her to turn so their eyes could meet; but the figure showed no sign of wanting to look round.

'Just as well the headland's blocking those rollers,' said Grandy, 'or she'd be washed straight off there.'

'Has anyone tried talking to her?' said Hetty.

'Lots of us,' said Grandy, 'but she won't answer, and Per's not helping things. He's been screaming abuse at her practically non-stop. It's bound to be putting her off trusting us. But we can't get him to shut up.'

Hetty saw the old man over to the right, peering out at the woman. His knuckles were white over the top of his stick. Mackie had now climbed onto the rocks and was trying to step out along the chain.

'Leave her, Mackie!' called Per. 'Leave her to die!'

Mackie shot a glance at him.

'I don't need your bile, old man.'

'Leave her to die! She's a jinx on the island!'

Mackie lost his footing. Isla gave a scream, but he wasn't in the water yet. He'd slid down the side of a boulder but had somehow managed to grab a rough edge and hold on, and now he was hauling himself back up. But the side of the boulder was slippery with slime and he was struggling to make progress. It was some minutes before he made it back to the top.

'Mackie!' called Isla. 'Come back.'

He looked round at her.

'It's too slippery,' she said, 'and you're too heavy.'

Mackie tested the next rock with his foot, then gave up and picked his way back to the beach. Per spat and hobbled up to him.

'See?'

'I'll tell you what I see,' said Mackie. 'I see a bitter old man who's lost his humanity and an old woman who needs our help.'

'She don't deserve our help,' spluttered Per, 'because she's the cause of all this. She brought the storm that wrecked *The Pride*, and she'll bring more evil if you let her.'

'You're a superstitious old fool.'

'I dreamt what I dreamt and I know what I know.'

Hetty ran forward and caught Per by the arm.

'She's a harmless old woman,' she said. 'She's not evil.'

As if she'd heard this, the woman suddenly turned and faced them again; and for the first time, Hetty met her eyes. The woman's expression changed at once: from wildness and terror to something fixed and intent. Without hesitation she took a step towards the shore.

'I don't believe it,' said Mackie.

Hetty ran closer to the rocks and stretched out her arms.

'Come on,' she called to the woman. 'Come back to the shore.'

The woman took another step, skidded slightly, but continued.

'Crawl,' Hetty called to her. 'It'll be safer. Come back on your hands and knees.'

The woman ignored this and continued to walk, slowly, shakily, her eyes never leaving Hetty's face. Hetty watched, hardly daring to believe that someone she had seen in the ghost of an image was now here in flesh and blood and moving towards her. The woman was halfway back now and still somehow hadn't stumbled. Hetty kept her arms outstretched, beckoning gently. But it was not to last.

'Go back where you came from!' shouted Per. 'We don't want you here!'

The woman stopped, took her eyes from Hetty and stared at the old man. He raised his stick and brandished it at her.

'Go back! Go back!'

The woman swayed, still staring at the old man.

'Go back!' he screamed.

'Stop it, Per!' said Hetty. 'She's my friend!'

'She ain't nobody's friend!' Per glared at the woman and screamed again. 'She's an enemy of this island and she's evil!'

The woman swayed again, her eyes still on Per, then plunged into the sea. Per gave a roar of triumph but it was quickly drowned by shouts from the others around the shore. Mackie kicked off his boots, tore off his coat and pullover, and ran into the shallows, Isla clinging to his arm.

'Don't, Mackie! It's too dangerous!'

He pushed her away and threw himself into the sea. Hetty stared in horror. The woman was floundering in the water and somehow keeping afloat, but she was still some way from the shore and it seemed impossible that Mackie would reach her in time. Per screamed again.

'Go back to the darkness, you witch!'

Hetty rounded on him, fists clenched.

'No, you go back, you sick old man!'

'Don't you tell me—'

'You go back!' she shouted. 'You're horrible! You're hateful!'

'You little—'

'You're evil!'

The old man raised his stick.

'Don't you dare hit me!' said Hetty.

Per brought the stick down hard. Hetty blocked it with one hand and thrust the old man away with the other. He tottered backwards but kept his footing somehow and stood there, glowering at her; then suddenly his face changed. His jaw tightened, his eyes hardened. He dropped his stick, his gaze never leaving her, and fell to the ground.

'Per's down!' someone shouted.

Lorna was there first, then Gregor and Harold, then a crowd of others.

'Give him air,' said Ailsa.

Hetty felt a hand pull her back. It was Grandy, looking grave.

'It was his fault, Grandy,' she said. 'He was trying to hit me.'

Grandy said nothing and simply pulled her further away. Hetty turned to the sea. The woman's head was still above the surface, but she was flailing her arms and clearly losing strength. Mackie was swimming powerfully towards her, but she was still out of reach. Suddenly she went under.

'No!' said Hetty.

She heard voices from the group tending Per.

'He's all right, he's all right.'

'Give him some room.'

'Easy, old boy.'

She kept her eyes on the water, and the empty space where the woman had been.

'Mackie!' called Isla. 'Come back! You won't reach her now!'

Mackie swam on. Isla started to wade out from the shore. Karl and Rory ran into the shallows and caught her by the arms, all three staring at Mackie. Suddenly he dived. Hetty held her breath, watching: nothing for several seconds, then a flurry of water and he burst into view again, the woman clutched to his shoulder. Her eyes were closed.

Isla pushed Karl and Rory away and started to swim out from the shore. The men dived after her, and a moment later Tam ran in too, and all four splashed their way out through the choppy water. With an immense effort Mackie drove himself towards them, pulling the woman with him. They closed round him, raised the woman's body a little higher, and then ploughed back together towards the shore.

Hetty studied the woman's face. It was blank and wet and still. Mackie and the others reached the shore and stood there in the shallows, panting. But there were few cheers; almost all the islanders were gathered round Per. Hetty stared at them for a moment, then turned back to the woman.

'Don't be dead,' she murmured. 'Please don't be dead.'

Isla and the men laid her down on the beach, and Grandy, Dolly, and Anna hurried over to examine her. Hetty reached into her pocket and squeezed the sea glass.

'You mustn't be dead,' she whispered to the woman. 'You came to find me.'

She heard a babble of talk around Per, then Grandy's voice close by.

'She's breathing but only just.'

Anna turned to Rory and Karl.

'Carry the woman to my cottage,' she said. 'Quick as you can. Spread this coat over her.'

But before the men could move, Gregor called across.

'There's someone else you should be thinking of,' he said. 'Someone more important than this miserable crone.'

He walked over to them, then turned to Hetty with a look of hatred.

'Per's dead,' he said.

# Chapter 10

They assembled in front of the chapel: the whole community apart from those inside preparing Per's body for burial, or those at Anna's cottage fighting to save the woman. Hetty glanced round. Tension hung over the group like a shroud, but what disturbed her most was the hostility: towards her.

She saw it in looks, shoulders turned, distance kept, not from everybody, but from a sizeable number. Even the Halvorson brothers and the boys from North Point were avoiding her eyes. Tam was standing next to her, though, with Mackie and Isla close by, and she was glad to have them there. She stared down the track at Anna's cottage, desperate to know what was happening inside.

'I wish Anna would let us in,' she said.

'There's no room,' said Tam. 'You know how cramped her cottage is.'

'They should have taken her to Moon Cottage. We've got plenty of space there.'

She felt Mungo and Duffy watching her. She turned sharply towards them and they looked away. Nessa and Jinty stared at her openly for a few moments, then glanced away too. Old Lorna stepped out of the chapel and shuffled over.

'So, Hetty,' she said, 'I hope you're pleased with yourself. The last words Per heard before he died were yours cursing him.' She glanced towards Anna's cottage. 'On behalf of . . . your friend.'

'Per cursed the woman first,' said Hetty.

'Maybe he had good reason to.'

'She's a harmless old woman who's been wrecked on our island.'

Lorna shrugged.

'You heard what he said about his dream.'

'Yes, and it was cruel.'

'But what if it was right?'

'What if it was wrong?'

Lorna didn't answer.

'He was talking superstitious rubbish,' said Hetty, 'and he was horrible to that woman. If he hadn't opened his mouth, she wouldn't have missed her footing and fallen in the sea.'

'If you hadn't opened yours, girl, Per would still be alive.'

Others were crowding round to listen.

'Lorna,' said Mackie, 'we all heard Per spouting. You did too.'

'But that's how Per was,' said Lorna, 'and none of us was ever going to change him. You know that as well as I do, Mackie. Hetty rounding on him and shoving him away was the worst thing she could have done. No wonder he had a heart attack.'

'He had a heart attack because he was old and ill,' said Mackie, 'not because of Hetty.'

Gregor and Harold pushed to the front.

'It was still wrong what Hetty done,' said Gregor. 'Like Lorna said, Per was never going to change and we all knew what he was like, every one of us. Maybe some of what he said down the years was a bit crazy, but some of it wasn't.'

'That's true,' said Lorna.

'And now he ain't here and we're stuck with that jinx instead, and all the bad luck she's brought us.' Gregor sniffed. 'And if Anna and Grandy bring her back to life, we're going to have a whole load more.'

'Per warned us about that too,' muttered Harold. 'Said there was going to be more evil because of that woman. Wasn't just about losing *The Pride*.'

'It's superstition,' said Hetty. 'Can't you see that?'

'You done wrong, girl,' said Gregor, 'simple as that, and you ain't doing yourself no favours piping up like this. You didn't show respect to Per, but you should have. He might have been difficult and I know he got bitter towards the end, but it don't excuse you snapping at him and pushing him and saying that woman's your friend when you ain't never seen her before.'

'Hetty has seen her before,' said Tam.

Gregor glanced at him.

'Is that so, young man?'

'Yes, it is,' said Tam. 'She told me she has and I believe her.'

'Well, good for you.' Gregor rolled his eyes at Lorna. 'Hetty's seen the woman before. Now I wonder where that could be. Let me guess.'

Hetty caught Tam's eye and saw him grimace.

'It's all right, Tam,' she said. 'I'm not ashamed of the sea glass.'

'You damn well should be,' said Lorna. 'You go on about Per being superstitious and then you claim to see faces in broken bottles. Now that really is stupid.'

'Totally infantile,' said Gregor. 'You can see faces in anything. It don't mean nothing. You can see 'em in clouds if you want to, or waves or sand or frost, or in the moon, or on misty windows, or turves of peat glowing in the fire.'

'Or poo,' said Hetty. 'Don't forget poo. You can see lots of faces in poo.'

She saw eyes harden around her.

'I don't care what you all think,' she said. 'Per was horrible to that woman.'

'Your friend,' sneered Mungo, somewhere behind her.

'Yes,' said Hetty, not looking round, 'my friend.'

The door of Anna's cottage opened and Grandy appeared. Harold grunted.

'Maybe your grandmother will knock some sense into you.'

Grandy walked slowly down to them.

'Is the woman still alive?' said Hetty.

Grandy didn't answer. She simply looked from face to face, then put a hand on Hetty's shoulder.

'Come with me,' she said quietly, and she steered Hetty towards the cottage.

'Grandy,' called Lorna.

Grandy stopped and looked round.

'We're burying Per this afternoon,' said Lorna. 'There'll be a service in the chapel.'

'I know.'

'That girl should be there to pay her respects.'

'She will be.'

And Grandy walked on, steering Hetty as before. At the door of the cottage she stopped again.

'Now, Hetty, listen—'

'I don't want a lecture.'

'You're not going to get a lecture.' Grandy lowered her voice. 'I've only brought you here to get you away from Lorna and the others.'

'Is the woman still alive?' said Hetty. 'You didn't answer my question.'

'She's alive,' said Grandy, 'but she's unconscious, in a deep place somewhere, maybe too deep to come back from. To be frank, Hetty, I don't rate her chances, and the others agree with me. I'm telling you this now because I don't want you to build up your hopes and then be upset later. Now listen . . . '

Grandy paused, frowning.

'Be very careful, Hetty.'

'You said you weren't going to give me a lecture.'

'Be very, very careful,' said Grandy. 'You're fired up and angry but you must watch what you say and do. You're not the most popular person on the island right now. I know you've never liked Per and his friends. Well, I'm not keen on them either and I agree Per behaved very badly with the woman, but he's been part of Mora longer than anybody else here, and for all his faults, there are people in this community who liked him—'

'I know that.'

'And some who even loved him. So you must put aside whatever anger you feel towards him and come with me to the burial service this afternoon.'

'Can I see the woman now?'

'All right.'

Anna's bedroom was dark and quiet. Anna and Dolly were standing by the bed, but they moved apart so that Grandy and Hetty could squeeze between them. Hetty stared down. The woman was lying on her back, blankets draped over her up to the neck. She looked dry and clean and her white hair had been brushed. Her eyes were closed, her body still.

Anna turned back the blankets for a moment to tidy the bottom sheet, and before she replaced them, Hetty caught a glimpse of the simple clothes they had found for the woman. The frame inside them was slight, the face

68

neither beautiful nor ugly, yet curiously arresting in this sculptured form. Again Hetty pondered the mystery of this woman's survival.

She looked round at the others and saw eyes closed, heads lowered, mouths moving silently. She did the same and summoned what prayers she could. The silence went on, broken only by the wind and the voices outside, and the howl of her own thoughts. Then she heard Dolly's voice.

'She doesn't want to come back.'

Hetty opened her eyes again and saw the others staring once more at the woman. Anna reached down and felt the pulse.

'Very faint,' she said after a moment. 'Fainter than last time.'

'She mustn't die,' said Hetty.

'We can't stop it happening,' said Grandy, 'if it's meant to be.'

'It's not meant to be,' said Hetty. 'She can't die here without her family or anyone knowing.'

The others looked at her, not unkindly.

'There's nothing we can do, Hetty,' said Anna. 'We don't know who she is or where she's come from, and even if we did, we haven't got a seagoing boat any more to carry news or find anything out. You know that as well as I do. Until we build a new boat, we're cut off, and so is this poor woman.'

'So what do we do?'

'We give her our care,' said Anna, 'and if it's not enough, we lay her next to Per in Mora's place of rest.'

'It's not right,' said Hetty. 'It's not what I saw.'

She squeezed the sea glass in her pocket and closed her eyes—then heard a cough. She blinked her eyes open again and leaned down, aware of the others doing the same. There was no change in the woman's face or body.

'The woman coughed,' she said.

'I know,' said Anna.

She reached under the blanket. Hetty waited, her eyes fixed on the still face.

'Pulse is a little stronger,' said Anna, 'but it's still weak.'

'Maybe our prayers are helping,' said Dolly.

'She still doesn't look close to coming back,' said Anna, 'yet there is a slight improvement.' She looked round the room. 'We could do with more space than this. If we're going to nurse her properly.'

'Grandy and I can take her,' said Hetty.

She saw the others turn to look at her.

'We've got the biggest cottage near here,' she said, 'and we've got a spare room, haven't we, Grandy?'

Grandy said nothing.

'We don't use it for anything,' said Hetty, 'and it's got a good bed, and there's a fireplace in the room—'

'Which hasn't been used for years,' said Grandy.

'It'll still work,' said Hetty. 'Please, Grandy, we can put the woman in there.'

Grandy frowned, then turned to Anna.

'We'll look after her at Moon Cottage,' she said. 'Hetty's right. We have got more space. But we'll have to be very careful how we move her. And we'll need some warmer clothing for her.'

'I can bring some things from the cottage,' said Hetty.

'No,' said Grandy, 'we'll sort that here. Go and see if Mackie's still outside. If he is, tell him we want two reliable people to carry the woman. Then run back to Moon Cottage and get things ready.'

Hetty hurried towards the door.

'Wait,' said Grandy. 'I haven't finished.'

Hetty stopped.

'We might be some time,' said Grandy. 'We can't move this woman quickly. Make sure there's a good fire in the main room, then check the old bedroom. Make up the bed in there and put plenty of blankets ready.'

'I can get a fire going in there too.'

'I'm not sure about that chimney. It hasn't been used for so long.'

'If it's smoky, we can put the woman in my bed.'

Grandy shook her head.

'If the old spare bedroom's no good, she'll sleep in mine, and if that's too cold, we'll make up a bed for her in the main room by the fire. Off you go. And make some vegetable soup. Chop everything very thin. We might just get something down her and she'll need it.'

Hetty ran out of the cottage and straight into Tam, who was standing just outside the door.

'What are you doing here?' she said.

'Waiting for you. Is the woman still alive?'

'Yes, but . . .'

She stared towards the chapel. The crowd was still there, and so was the hostility. She looked back at Tam.

'I saw that woman, Tam. I saw her in the sea glass.'

'I believe you,' said Tam. He hesitated. 'Have you got it with you?'

'Yes.'

'Can I see it?'

She pulled out the sea glass and held it up. The dark form was still there, clear and strong. Tam stared into it.

'Can you see the shape of the face?' said Hetty.

Tam narrowed his eyes and went on staring. She watched him for a moment, then shook her head.

'You can't, can you?'

'I'm sorry, Hetty. I'm really trying to.'

'I know you are, Tam. It's all right.'

She pulled the glass back and looked at it herself, then gave a start. The shape had changed within the last minute. The face that had seemed so well defined now looked distorted. She pictured the face of the woman inside the cottage and frowned; but there was no time to ponder this now. She thrust the sea glass back in her pocket.

'Mackie!' she called.

Mackie came hurrying over.

'What's going on, Hetty?'

'They're going to move the woman to Moon Cottage. I've got to run on ahead to get things ready. Grandy's looking for two people to carry her.'

'That's easy enough.'

'I can help,' said Tam.

'Good lad,' said Mackie. 'We'll manage it between us.'

And he and Tam disappeared inside the cottage. Hetty hurried off down the track, hoping she wouldn't have to speak to anyone from the crowd; but as she drew near, Gregor called out to her.

'That woman still breathing?'

She stopped and looked at him.

'Yes,' she said.

The old man glanced at Harold and grunted. Lorna stepped alongside them.

'Make sure you come to Per's burial service, girl,' she muttered.

And before Hetty could answer, the three of them turned away.

# Chapter 11

Hetty raced to the top of the rise and stared down at the sea. The wind had lost none of its malign force and the waves were still crashing into the bay. A haunted sun drifted among the clouds. She ran on, pictures of the woman's face flooding her mind, and with them the distorted image she'd just seen in the sea glass: a deathly image. She cut right, under the shoulder of the hill, and stopped, the sound of the surf heavy below her. She looked down at the grey-white mane tumbling on the shore.

'I saw you in the sea glass,' she said to the woman, 'and you were alive. Your eyes were open and you were staring out at me.'

Thunder rolled in the distance and a moment later lightning flashed over the western cliffs. She raced on and didn't stop until she had reached Moon Cottage. The main room was cold but she built up the fire and coaxed it into life, then walked through into the old empty bedroom. It felt strange to be in this unused place. She'd sometimes wondered whether spirits lived here, but she'd never felt any, and certainly not her mother and father.

She made up the bed, found some extra blankets, then stared at the dusty fireplace. She'd never once seen a fire burning in it. Perhaps Grandy was right and the chimney was too dirty to use. It was probably best to make the soup first. But it was no good. She knew what she wanted. She fetched some turves of peat, prepared the fire as carefully as she could, and lit it. There was a crackle, then another, and finally a small flame.

She watched, her mind on the woman's face as she wanted to see it here in this room: awake, alive, aware of her. The flame died, but only for a new one to burst out, larger and brighter. The crackle grew louder and the rich, peaty smell began to spread. She reached out with the poker and prodded the fire into a better shape. The flames spread greedily and smoke snaked up through the chimney. She heard voices outside the cottage and thought of the unmade soup. Grandy would chide her for not having started it.

She paused even so, half-listening to the voices, half to the storm, which somehow had slipped from her conscious mind and was now back again, then she pulled out the sea glass and held it before the fire. The flames shot towards it in deep slanting rays that seemed to pierce through the glass and into her. She stared at the dark shape, still present, still a face, but ever more distorted; and a flicker of fear passed through her.

'What's happening to you?' she said to the woman.

The door of the cottage opened with a bang, hastened by the wind. She thrust the sea glass back in her pocket and hurried to the door of the room. Grandy was walking slowly towards her. Behind her came Anna and Dolly, and then Mackie and Tam carrying the woman on an improvised stretcher. She was wrapped in blankets and propped up with cushions. Her eyes were still closed.

'Wait,' said Grandy to the others.

They stopped with the stretcher just beyond the threshold of the room. Grandy walked in, looking about her.

'The fire's all right, Grandy,' said Hetty. 'Not smoky, see?'

Grandy studied it for a few moments, then looked over the bed.

'I've made it up ready,' said Hetty.

Grandy checked it over with the same solemnity, then turned to the others.

'Bring her through.'

They carried the woman in. Hetty stood aside, her eyes on the woman's face. It was horribly pale.

'Can I do something, Grandy?' she said.

'Keep an eye on the fire.'

She nursed it for a while, resisting the urge to look round. Behind her she could hear the soft movements as the woman was eased from the stretcher into the bed, the sheets and blankets smoothed over her, the footsteps as the others moved about. When she finally looked round, Mackie and Tam had gone, and Anna, Dolly, and Grandy were standing there, praying. The woman was propped up in bed, cushions under her head and back. She was breathing quietly, but as before there was no sign of movement or awareness of those around her. Grandy opened her eyes.

'Soup, Hetty.'

Hetty jumped to her feet.

'Sorry, I should have started it.'

'You're doing fine, Hetty,' said Anna.

'Thin as possible,' said Grandy, 'like I told you. And then you must get ready for Per's burial service.'

'I don't want to go.'

'There's no argument about it,' said Grandy. 'We're both going.'

'Someone's got to look after the woman.'

'Anna and Dolly are staying,' said Grandy. 'We agreed that on the way here. Everybody knows someone's got to look after the woman. Everybody will understand why it's Anna and Dolly. Nobody will understand you not being at Per's burial service.'

'But—'

'Mackie and Tam have gone off to get ready,' said Grandy. 'You're going to do the same. But get the soup started first.'

Hetty scowled, but she could see Grandy was not for shifting. She hurried out of the room and started chopping vegetables, aware once again of the wind and the surf, and her mounting anger. For all the guilt that was secretly playing upon her over Per's death, she could not escape the pictures of the old man's snapping face, his stick stabbing the air as he spat his vicious words at the woman, and her plunge into the sea, perhaps to her own death. She worked on, glad to be alone for the moment, and soon the soup was cooking. She left it for a short while and wandered over to the window. The sea was still a turbulence of white all the way to the horizon.

'Ghost water,' she murmured to it, 'how can you be so beautiful and so cruel?'

She returned to the soup, tasted it and added some seasoning. The door to the spare room opened and Grandy stepped out.

'Is the soup ready?'

'Yes.'

'Nice and thin?'

'See for yourself.'

Grandy walked over, dipped a spoon and tasted the soup.

'Very good,' she said. 'How can you cook so well and not like eating?'

'How's the woman?'

'You didn't answer my question.'

'I'm not going to,' said Hetty. 'How's the woman?'

'No different from the last time you saw her,' said Grandy. 'It's hard to know whether it was a good idea

76

bringing her here or not. I know she coughed earlier and her pulse got a tiny bit better, but she looks more gaunt and pale since she arrived here, and her pulse has gone back to what it was. Very, very faint.'

'When do you think she last ate or drank?'

'No idea,' said Grandy. 'She could have been days at sea.'

'Did you get anything down her at Anna's place?'

'Not really. A dribble of water maybe, and most of it went down her front. But we'll have to get her to eat and drink soon or she'll waste away. It's a miracle she's survived this long. Let's put some of this soup in a mug.'

'I've warmed one ready.'

'Good girl.' Grandy filled the mug and picked up a small spoon. 'I'll take this too. Anna and Dolly might just be able to feed her tiny bits with it while you and I are getting ready for Per's service.'

'Grandy—'

'Don't start all over again,' said Grandy. 'You need to be at the burial service and that's all there is to it. It'll be seen as a mark of great disrespect if you're not there, so go and get changed into your best things. Smart as you can. I'll do the same, after I've taken the soup through. Meet me back here when you're ready. And make it quick or we'll be late. No more than five minutes.'

But it was fifteen by the time they set off down the track.

'Dawdling won't stop you going to the service,' said Grandy.

'I'm not dawdling.'

'Yes, you are,' said Grandy, 'just like you took your time dressing. Don't think I didn't notice. But it makes no difference, girl. You're going to the service whether you like it or not, and if we arrive after they've started, I'm shoving you in through the door ahead of me.'

But even as they walked, Hetty knew she wasn't going. All she could think of was the woman at Moon Cottage; and the man who had probably killed her. They reached the track that branched off in the direction of the chapel—and she stopped.

'It's no good, Grandy.'

'Hetty—'

'I'm not going.'

Grandy opened her mouth to speak, then closed it again. Hetty looked round and saw figures hurrying towards them, all in their best clothes. Grandy nodded to them all as they passed, then turned to Hetty again.

'You mustn't miss the service, Hetty.'

'Did you see how they looked at me?'

'I don't think they even noticed you,' said Grandy. 'They were too worried about being late for the service. As you should be.'

'They sneered at me,' said Hetty. 'I'm not imagining it. You said yourself I'm unpopular and I can see it in people's faces. They hate me. I know I rounded on Per, but he was spiteful and horrible, and he frightened the woman and made her slip, and now she's in a coma because of him, and she might not come back.'

'I know that.'

'And she was nearly there, Grandy! She nearly made it back to the shore!'

'I know,' said Grandy. 'Per was wrong. I'm not saying he wasn't.' She gave a sigh. 'And I didn't say you're unpopular. I said you're not the most popular person on the island right now. That's not the same thing.'

'Doesn't sound very different to me.'

Grandy took her hand.

'Hetty, nobody hates you on the island, but some people are angry because they think you behaved rashly with Per, and I'm worried that if you don't pay the old man your respects now, you might provoke something worse.'

'I can't do it, Grandy,' said Hetty. 'I'm just too angry with him.'

She saw another figure approaching, this time from the direction of the chapel. It was Lorna.

'I was just coming to find you two,' she said coldly. She looked Hetty over. 'But now the girl's here, we can start the service.'

'I'm not coming, Lorna,' said Hetty.

'Why not?'

'Because that woman could have lived,' said Hetty, 'and now she's probably going to die, and it's all because of Per. I'll never forgive him for that.'

And with a last look at Grandy, she bolted down the track. She tore past Broken Tooth Ridge and Holm Edge and up the eastern side of the island, running hard. To her right the sea brayed and billowed under the chasing clouds. She paused at the top of Skull Cove, fighting to catch her breath, and then she was running again. She didn't stop till she'd reached the north-eastern extremity of Snag Head. Below her the rocks were awash with foam as the waves continued to batter the island. Sheep wandered about her, munching quietly.

She sat down among them, still angry.

It was late in the afternoon when she returned to Moon Cottage. No one was in the main room but she could hear Grandy, Anna, and Dolly talking in low voices behind the closed door of the spare room. She knelt in front of the fire and pulled the sea glass from her pocket again. The distorted shape was still locked inside it, unwilling as yet to give up its secret. She held the glass towards the flames and they seemed to crackle over it, brightening and darkening the image as the light played and died.

She leaned closer suddenly, aware of a new mystery. The shape was still there but it seemed to be splitting in two, and now each misty form was transmuting itself into a distinct entity. She drew back, frightened of these new transfigurations. The flames crackled on, hot on her extended hand. She pictured the woman's face beyond the door, then stared again at the sea glass. Nowhere in the two forms was the image of the woman she had once seen there.

'You're not her any more,' she said to them. 'So who are you? Or what?'

The door to the spare room opened and she saw Anna standing there.

'Hetty,' she said, 'I didn't hear you come back.'

'Is the woman any better?'

'No change, I'm afraid.'

'Did you get any soup down her?'

Anna shook her head. Hetty looked down again.

'That's a nice piece of sea glass,' said Anna.

'Don't make fun of me.'

'I'm not making fun of you, Hetty.'

'I know you all think I'm stupid about this.'

Anna walked across and knelt down.

'I don't think that, Hetty,' she said. 'I really don't. Can I look at the sea glass? Can I hold it?'

Hetty hesitated.

'I won't if it's sacred,' said Anna.

'It's just that . . .'

'I promise I'm not making fun of you,' said Anna. 'I know the sea glass is important to you. Look, I won't take it from you. I don't think I should touch it. I just wanted to look into it. But I don't have to do that either, not if you don't want me to.'

Hetty held up the sea glass.

'Can you see the shapes?'

Anna peered into the glass.

'I can see the smoothness of the glass,' she said, 'and how clear and beautiful it is, and I can see the flames from the fire pushing through it. Are those the shapes you mean?'

Hetty looked away.

'Don't be angry with me,' said Anna. 'You can see things I can't. That's all.'

The fire spat at their feet. Anna tidied the embers and stood up.

'You're so tensed up, Hetty,' she said. 'But you don't have to fight any of us here, remember.'

'Sorry, Anna.'

'It's all right.'

'Can I see the woman?'

'Of course you can.'

They made their way through to the spare room. Grandy and Dolly were standing by the bed. The woman lay propped up as before, her head turned away. Her breathing had slowed almost to nothing. The mouth and eyes were closed, the features still, and there was a desolation in the face that Hetty had not seen before.

'What's going to happen?' she said.

Grandy turned to her.

'Anna, Dolly, and I will sit with her in shifts.'

'I can help too.'

'No,' said Grandy, 'you can go and eat some of the food I've left out for you, and then you can spend the rest of the evening cleaning the cottage.'

'I want to help with the woman, Grandy.'

'I'm sure you do,' said Grandy, 'but she doesn't need four of us in her present state. The cottage, however, needs cleaning and it won't happen on its own. I'll come out later and make sure you've eaten all the food.'

Hetty stared at the woman, then back at her grand-mother; and she knew there was no point in arguing this time. She set off towards the door, then stopped and turned.

'The burial service,' she said, 'was it—'

'You were missed,' said Grandy.

# Chapter 12

Morning showed no diminution in the storm. Hetty stared out of her bedroom window at the wild sea and the racing clouds. If anything, conditions seemed to be getting worse. She dressed, splashed her face with water and crept to the spare room. No sounds came from within. She eased open the door and peeped through.

The woman was lying in the bed, eyes closed, body still. She seemed as unreachable as ever. Anna and Dolly had not yet arrived for their first shift, but Grandy was dozing in the chair nearby. Hetty closed the door, hurried past the breakfast that her grandmother had left out for her, and pulled on her coat and boots. Then she opened the door of the cottage and stepped out.

A gust knocked her straight back in, but she staggered through, closed the door behind her and tramped off down the path towards the bay. She hoped desperately that she wouldn't meet anyone on the way, even those who didn't look upon her as a girl in disgrace. It was one thing having to face people like Lorna and Gregor, neither of whom she'd ever cared for, but quite another to see people she loved like Mackie and Isla sticking up for her and getting into arguments on her account. That was almost too much to bear.

And she didn't want to see Tam. She definitely didn't want to see Tam.

She soon realized, however, that she was not going to be alone on the shingle beach. Mungo and Duffy were there ahead of her. She stopped on the path and for a moment considered hiding somewhere till they'd gone.

'Act strong,' she told herself.

She walked on, squalls punching into her, and stopped at the quay. Before her the water foamed and fumed. Crab Rock was white; so was Eel Point. The inshore rocks upon which *The Pride of Mora* had impaled herself were submerged and rollers were driving over them onto the shore. She scanned the shingle beach, half-hoping Mungo and Duffy might have scrambled up the farther track towards High Crag.

But the boys were still there, throwing stones into the surf. She watched them for a few minutes, wondering whether they'd spotted her. She sensed that they had, though neither looked her way. She set off down the path that ran along the top of the beach towards the spot where the dinghies had been pulled up.

The boys went on throwing stones and she began to hope they were going to ignore her, but the moment she reached the row of dinghies and started to make her way down it, they came running up the shingle. She pretended not to notice and walked on to *Baby Dolphin*. One glance was enough to see that the little boat was undamaged.

She'd been worried about the mast, sail, and yard but they were lashed down inside the dinghy as securely as when she'd left them. There were several inches of water in the bottom, however. She pushed aside the thought of the boys and felt under the thwart for the baler. A few moments later a hand appeared over her shoulder. She glanced at it.

'Very funny, Mungo,' she said.

He was holding a piece of sea glass close to her eyes. She let go of the baler and straightened up to see both boys grinning at her. Mungo pushed the sea glass at her.

'We've been staring into it,' he said, 'but we can't see any faces. Duffy thought maybe you could.'

Duffy sniggered. Hetty looked at him, then back at Mungo, who was watching her with mock-earnestness.

'Can you have a look at it, Hetty?' he said. 'You're bound to see something in it. Since you've got this . . . you know . . . '

'Special gift,' said Duffy.

The two boys exchanged glances. Hetty took the sea glass from Mungo. It was a blurry, salt-encrusted thing with a slightly pointed end. She felt a great yearning to stick it in Mungo's face and punch it in deep. She took a slow breath, reached down into *Baby Dolphin* and washed the sea glass in some of the water that had collected in the bottom of the dinghy, then she straightened up again and wiped it dry on Mungo's sleeve.

'Thanks very much,' he said.

She studied the glass with the same mock-earnestness he had shown her. It was an unspectacular piece and she felt sure it would never yield anything worth looking at, even if she'd wanted to try. She went on playing the game, however.

'I can see something,' she said eventually.

'Yeah?' said Mungo.

'A face.' She held the glass up. 'See it?'

Mungo gave it a token glance.

'You're not looking properly,' she said.

She held it closer to his eyes.

'Now do you see it?'

He didn't answer.

'What's wrong with you?' she said. 'Are you blind?'

She held it up to Duffy.

'You look,' she said. 'Since he can't. Go on. Look hard.'

Duffy glanced at Mungo.

'Don't look at Mungo,' said Hetty. 'Look at the sea glass.'

Duffy looked at the glass.

'Can't you see the face?' she said.

Duffy shrugged. She gave a snort.

'You're both blind,' she said. 'It's easy, look.'

She held the sea glass up to the sky. Through it came a distorted grey tinged with the white of the clouds.

'You can't miss it,' she said. 'Look, Mungo, it's got . . . brown hair, really scrawny, snotty hair and . . . two boring pale blue eyes and . . . a kind of horrible lopsided mouth. It's a boy about fifteen years old and he's so . . . '

'Yeah, yeah,' said Mungo.

'So ugly,' she went on, 'God, he's gross, Mungo. No girl in her right mind would go for a boy like that.'

'Yeah, all right. I get it. See you around.'

'No wait,' she said. 'I can see another face.'

The boys started to move off towards the quay. She shouted after them.

'Duffy, look at this one! He's even more gross. Do you want me to tell you about him?'

'Don't bother,' called Duffy.

'I can if you want!'

No answer.

'Oh, please!' she yelled. 'Let me tell you about the other face!'

She went on screaming after them, but they didn't stop. She felt a flutter of satisfaction at the sight of them trying—and failing—to saunter, but then they were gone, and so was the pleasure of hurting them. All that remained was a new layer of guilt. She threw the sea glass away and found she was trembling. She leaned on the gunwale of *Baby Dolphin*.

'I shouldn't try to act strong,' she said to the boat.

She pulled out the baler and scooped away as much water as she could, then wiped round with a cloth. It felt good to be alone with her boat, but she was still trembling. She heard steps behind her on the shingle and whirled round, fists clenched.

Tam was standing there.

'You all right, Hetty?'

'Why wouldn't I be?'

'You look like you've just been in a fight.' He hesitated. 'Or you're looking for one.'

She unclenched her fists and waited for her breathing to slow down.

'You startled me, that's all,' she said.

'I didn't mean to.'

He stood there awkwardly, the wind blowing his hair over his face. She considered him for a moment, trying to see the old Tam, the one she had known for so many years. But all had changed in the last few months; and with his growing physical strength he was looking more and more like his father, though Mackie's hair was thinning.

'What do you want, Tam?' she said.

She hated the tone of her voice: so hard and remote. But it was the only voice she had right now.

'Do I have to want something to come and see you?' he said.

'I don't know.' She glanced over *Baby Dolphin*. 'I just thought . . . you maybe came down for a reason.'

'I have got a reason.'

She looked quickly round at him.

'Are you holding something behind your back?'

'Yes,' he said.

'What is it?'

'The reason.'

'Tam, can you get to the point?'

'The woman you're nursing at Moon Cottage,' he said. 'She's from the mainland.'

With something of a flourish he pulled his secret from behind his back. It was a small, flat, rectangular piece of wood.

'I was exploring in Skull Cove,' he said, 'and I found this. It was caught in some seaweed by those rocks where we saw the wreckage floating. It's the name board from that woman's boat. It can't be anything else. Same wood, same place where the boat got smashed.'

She saw him watching for her reaction; but all she could do was take the name board and read it.

SEMPER FIDELIS
HAGA

She frowned. Haga was a familiar enough name: the northernmost port on the mainland, though only Mackie and his trading crews had ever been there. The other words were strange.

'What's *Semper Fidelis*?' she said.

'The name of the boat.'

'But what does it mean?'

'Don't ask me,' said Tam. 'But the point is the boat's from Haga. So that woman's probably from there too. And you know what it also means?'

Again she saw him watching for her reaction.

'What does it mean?' she said, though she knew the answer.

'It means she's travelled over fifty miles to get here,' he said. 'Through that storm, in that boat. You remember what you said to me? About how you think she came here to find you?'

'You think that's stupid, don't you?'

'I think it's amazing.'

Tam smiled at her, and this time she managed a smile back.

'I've got a second reason for being here,' he said.

She felt her smile fade.

'What's that?' she said, somewhat warily.

'To see if you're going to the meeting.'

'What meeting?'

'Gregor's called it,' he said. 'An emergency meeting. They'll be starting in about half an hour. Rory came to tell Father about it. Didn't someone call at Moon Cottage for Grandy?'

'I didn't see anyone.'

'You probably just missed them when you went out,' said Tam. 'Anyway, there's a meeting and I wanted to know if you're going.'

'Is it for the whole community?'

'No, just Elders.'

'So we're not allowed.'

'We can listen in, can't we?'

Hetty saw the mischief in his eyes, together with the other thing: the thing she wished he didn't feel. She looked away, her mind on the woman from Haga, and then Tam again, and her fear of hurting him.

'How are we going to listen in?' she said.

'Leave that to me,' said Tam. 'Come on.'

They scrambled up the shingle beach and set off down the path to the quay.

'I saw Mungo and Duffy,' he said. 'They told me you were down here.'

She waited for him to say more, but he remained silent. They reached the track that curled up the side of the cliff and started to climb. At Broken Tooth Ridge they stopped to catch their breath, then Tam began to move on. Hetty caught him by the arm.

'Why do you hang around with Mungo and Duffy?'

'Why not?'

'They're idiots.'

Tam shrugged.

'What choice have I got? You keep avoiding me these days.'

'I'm not avoiding you,' she said.

But he turned and ran off down the path. She raced after him but he put on speed and wouldn't let her catch up till they'd reached the meeting hall. The main door was closed but from inside came a babble of voices. Tam was already moving round the side of the building. Hetty caught him by the arm again.

'I'm not avoiding you, Tam.'

He didn't answer.

'I'm not,' she said.

But she could tell from his eyes that he sensed the lie.

'I'll show you how to listen in,' he said, and he led her round to the little door at the back of the building. 'Here.'

'The privy?'

'Yes.'

'I'm not going in there.'

'Why not?' said Tam. 'It's perfect. The meeting room's right next door and the wall's really thin.'

'Have you done this before?'

'Haven't you?'

'No.'

'Well, it's your choice,' said Tam.

And he stepped inside and closed the door after him. Hetty stood there, unsure what to do; then she heard Grandy's voice, and a moment later, Anna's, both women approaching the meeting hall from further down the track. She squeezed the sea glass in her pocket, her mind once again on the woman from Haga. The voices drew nearer. She hesitated, then opened the door to the privy, and slipped in.

# *Chapter 13*

'Lock the door,' said Tam. 'In case someone comes.'

She locked the door, somewhat reluctantly, then turned and leaned her back against it. The privy was dark and foul-smelling, but there was just room for the two of them to stand without their bodies touching. The storm seemed strangely remote and she quickly realized that Tam was right: the sounds from the meeting room penetrated the wall easily.

She could hear every voice, and it was clear that all the Elders were present apart from Grandy, Anna, and Dolly. It was also clear that the meeting had not yet started. Then she heard the main door open and close, and Grandy's voice.

'Sorry we couldn't get here sooner. Have we missed much?'

'You ain't missed nothing,' said Gregor. 'We was waiting for you to arrive before we started. Where's Dolly? We need all the Elders here.'

'She's sitting with the woman,' said Grandy.

'Can't Hetty do that?' said Gregor. 'I'd have thought she'd want to.' He gave a scornful laugh. 'Since the woman's her special friend.'

'No need for that, Gregor,' said Grandy.

'I agree,' said Mackie, 'and we don't have to have all the Elders here either. One missing won't spoil the meeting. As you well know, old man.'

Hetty saw Tam lean closer.

'They're at each other already,' he whispered.

'So, Gregor,' said Anna, 'you called the meeting.'

'Yes, I did,' said the old man briskly, 'because it seems to me some of you have forgotten what's important. And since poor old Per's no longer with us, God rest him, seems it's up to me to knock sense into some of you.'

No one interrupted him.

'First point,' he went on, 'we've lost *The Pride* and we got to build another boat, and we got to do it quick or we ain't going to be able to trade before winter sets in. Simple as that. It couldn't be more urgent.'

'Listen—' said Mackie.

'No, you listen, Mackie,' said Gregor, 'because I ain't finished. You can talk when I'm done.'

'Have it your own way.'

'We got stock piled up ready to go to Brinda and the other islands,' said the old man, 'and it's just sitting there. What's the point of having prime wool and rare stone on Mora and our people working their fingers to the bone spinning and knitting and weaving and chipping our ornaments if we ain't trading nothing?'

'Can I talk now?' said Mackie.

'No, you can't,' said Gregor. 'I'll tell you when it's your turn and it ain't yet.'

There was a buzz of voices that flared and then faded back to silence. Hetty saw Tam look at her and frown. Gregor thundered on.

'We're struggling already with fish stocks low and our last harvest so bad, so we got to focus on building the new boat now.'

'Gregor,' said Mackie, 'you talk like the rest of us don't know all this. Of course we're going to build a new boat, and she'll be as good as *The Pride*. We've got the resources and we've got the skills, and I'm going to organize a working party the moment the storm goes down.'

'But it ain't the storm that's stopping you, Mackie,' said Gregor. 'It's this damn woman. And that was my second point, if you hadn't gone and interrupted me. All you and your people are thinking about is looking after this woman, when she's the cause of all our problems in the first place. Per gave us fair warning and it turns out he was right.'

'I agree,' said Lorna.

There was another buzz of talk round the room. In the little privy, Hetty glowered at the connecting wall, anger rising within her. Tam leaned close again.

'Don't shout through at them,' he whispered.

'I'm not going to,' she whispered back.

But it was hard.

'We shouldn't be helping that old crone,' Gregor went on. 'We should let her waste away. We've already lost *The Pride* because of her. Who's to say what evil she'll bring next if we give her the chance? I'm telling you, Per was right. She ain't no normal castaway. She's a jinx.'

'She's not a jinx,' said Mackie.

'She is,' said Gregor. 'I know what I'm talking about.'

'Don't tell me you had a dream about it like Per.'

'I don't need no dream to tell me when someone's trouble.'

'And what do you need, old man?'

'My experience,' said Gregor, 'and I got forty more years of it than you have, Mackie. I've sailed with men who brought bad luck and I know what they're like. Your father would back me over this if he was alive. And I've known women too what brought the same kind of trouble.'

'Everybody's crops failed,' said Lorna, 'when that half-sister of Freda's came to live on Mora. Some of you are old enough to remember her. I had a bad feeling about that woman the moment she arrived. And soon as she went, the crops picked up again.'

94

'They would have failed anyway,' said Grandy. 'It was nothing to do with Freda's half-sister, and it's the same with this woman from the sea. She's been unlucky enough to find herself adrift in a small boat and wrecked on our island. But she's not responsible for the storm that destroyed *The Pride*.'

'She's taken over your mind,' said Gregor.

'She's taken over yours,' said Grandy. 'She's a harmless old woman but all you and Lorna want to do is make things up about her.'

'Go round the island,' said Gregor, 'and talk to people like I been doing. They'll all tell you they don't trust this woman. Per had it right all along. And don't you go lecturing me about making things up, Grandy, when you got young Hetty with her rubbish about faces in sea glass, and her rounding on Per like she did and cursing him to his face, and then refusing to come to the chapel and pay her last respects to him. She's out of control, that girl.'

'And she's getting worse,' said Lorna. 'She was down on the beach screaming this morning. I was getting ready to leave my cottage and I heard her over the wind and the surf. Standing by her dinghy, she was, screaming her head off at nothing and nobody. Explain that to me, Grandy.'

'Hetty's got good reason to scream,' said Grandy, 'and good reason to look for faces.'

'In sea glass?' said Gregor.

'In anything she wants,' said Grandy. 'You might do the same if you had her history.'

'I got my own history,' the old man muttered.

'Good for you,' said Grandy. 'Then leave Hetty to hers. As for the woman, you can all stop worrying. Dolly, Anna, and I are agreed she won't last another day.'

Hetty reached for the privy door, unable to listen any more. She felt Tam's hand on her shoulder, threw him an angry glance, and he drew it back. She unlocked the door, pushed it open and ran away down the track, not looking behind. At the top of the rise she saw Mungo and Duffy watching her.

'Don't say anything,' she snarled at them. 'Just don't.'

They stared at her as she raced past. She tore down to High Crag, scrambled to the top, and sat there, braced against the wind. Below her, the sea rolled and smashed against the shore. She stared down at it, crying, her hand tight round the sea glass in her pocket. It was some hours before Tam found her again. She went on watching the turmoil of the sea.

'You're shivering,' he said.

She didn't answer. He sat down beside her and put an arm round her. She leaned into him slightly. He kissed the side of her head and she moved apart again.

'Sorry,' he said, taking his arm away.

'We've failed her, Tam,' she said. 'That woman. We've failed her. I've failed her.'

'You haven't failed her, Hetty.'

'I have.' She looked at him. 'She came here to find me. I know you must think that's crazy—'

'I don't think it's crazy, Hetty. I told you earlier.'

Tam reached into his pocket and pulled out two bread rolls. Hetty stared at them.

'Dolly's finest,' he said. 'She brought some to Moon Cottage and Grandy asked me to give these to you if I found you.'

'Did she ask you to come looking for me?'

'Yes.'

'I'm sorry.'

'It's all right,' said Tam. 'I was looking for you anyway. I've been up and down the island. I ran up the east side and round Snag Head and North Point and down to Hermit's Grotto and places I know you like, but you weren't at any of them, so I called at Moon Cottage to see if you'd gone home. I wasn't expecting to find you there, but Grandy was back from the meeting, and she was worried about you, and so was I, so I came out again. Should have come to High Crag first, I suppose. Did you come straight here from the meeting hall?'

'Yes.'

Tam shrugged.

'Ah, well.'

'It's really good of you,' she said. 'Looking out for me like that.'

He handed her the rolls.

'You'd better take these,' he said. 'Grandy said you probably wouldn't eat them, but she said I was to give them to you in case.'

Hetty took them without a word, turned back to the sea, and ate distractedly. A few moments later she felt Tam's arm slip round her again. She let it stay there and finished the rolls, then turned and looked at him again.

'Thanks, Tam,' she said quietly.

She stood up.

'I've got to go now.'

# *Chapter 14*

The woman lay exactly as Hetty had last seen her: eyes closed, face still. Grandy, Anna, and Dolly stood round the bed in silence. Hetty spoke from the doorway.

'Did Tam tell you she's from the mainland?'

All three looked round at her.

'No, he didn't,' said Grandy. 'How does he know that?'

'He found the name board from her boat. It's from Haga.'

'Well, that settles it,' said Grandy. 'The people of Haga don't come to us any more, and since we don't have a boat to go to them, this woman's going to die on Mora.'

Hetty walked up to the bed, her eyes on the woman's face.

'Don't speak so loud, Grandy,' she murmured. 'She can hear.'

Dolly leaned close.

'Hetty,' she said in a low voice, 'you can't change things, I'm afraid. This woman's story is nearly over. Whatever happened to bring her to Mora, it's broken her and she's dying.'

'She's not.'

'She is, sweetheart.'

'Dolly's right, Hetty,' said Anna, also in a low voice. 'We've seen too many people die here down the years. I wish we hadn't, but this is Mora. The woman is moving on now, and if she's conscious of anything, she's conscious of that.'

Hetty sat on the edge of the bed and took the woman's hand. It felt cold and brittle.

'Leave me with her,' she said.

'No, Hetty,' said Grandy. 'Let it be now.'

Hetty closed her other hand round the woman's.

'I'm not moving, Grandy.'

'Hetty—'

'If you want me to leave, you'll have to find Mackie and get him to carry me away.'

'Don't be stubborn.'

'I get my stubbornness from you, Grandy.'

Anna and Dolly exchanged glances. Grandy looked at them.

'Maybe it's best if—'

'We'll wait outside, Grandy,' said Anna.

The two women left. Grandy closed the door after them and walked back to the bed.

'Move up a bit,' she said.

Hetty stayed where she was.

'Move up, girl,' said Grandy. 'There's room for both of us to sit there, and you don't have to let go of the woman's hand.'

'I'm not going to,' said Hetty.

But she did move, just a few inches, still cradling the woman's hand, and now stroking the forearm—also cold, also brittle, but not dead, not yet. She sensed a whisper of life still present. She slid one hand over the woman's wrist and felt for the pulse, aware of Grandy watching.

'Hardly a beat, see?' said Grandy.

'I don't care,' said Hetty. 'I'm still staying. I just want to help, and I think I can.'

'What are you going to do?'

99

'Sit with her,' said Hetty. 'That's all. What harm can it do? You and Anna and Dolly haven't done any better. And you three are the best healers on Mora.'

'We lose more than we save.'

Grandy gazed over the little room, the empty cupboards and shelves, the rickety bedside table, the fire burning in the grate. The only brightness here.

'So many dead, Hetty,' she went on. 'They swim around us here on Mora, and you know that better than anybody. But we can't bring them back, girl. All we can do is help the living as best we can.'

'That's all I want too,' said Hetty.

Grandy stood up, walked over to the fire and poked it, then turned back to the bed.

'Someone should sit with her as she dies,' she said, 'and it might just as well be you. I'll be outside. Call me when you get tired. Or if anything happens.'

'Don't worry about me.'

'I do worry about you, Hetty. I worry about you all the time.'

And Grandy left the room. From beyond the closed door came the sound of her footsteps moving away, then silence—and then the wind. Hetty listened to it, wondering not for the first time how she could forget the gale so easily and then notice it again; how silence and storm could co-exist. Yet the wind and the silence went on, each so pervasive in their separate characters that at times she found it hard to know which was where: sometimes the silence seemed outside the cottage and the storm within, then the roles were reversed and the wind returned to its domain.

She fell back into the stillness of the room. All that broke it was the hiss and crackle of the fire. The breathing of the woman was too faint to hear; almost too faint to

100

believe in. She ran her eyes over the unmoving face. The features seemed frozen. She stroked the hand, the arm, the shoulder, then leaned down and whispered.

'Live.'

She touched the woman's neck.

'Please let me do this,' she said. 'I promise I won't hurt you.'

The wind returned, and then the silence, and then both. She rested her hand on the quiet cheek. Nothing moved in the face, but she felt the coldness of the skin subside a little, as though some of her warmth had reached through.

'You must be so thirsty.'

She took her hand away and looked round. A glass of water sat on the bedside table. She dipped a finger in it and traced the wet tip over the woman's lips. They did not move. She dipped her finger again and brought it back to the woman's lips. Again they did not respond. She eased the tip round the cheeks, over the chin, dipped two fingers and went on moistening the skin, whispering all the time into the woman's ear.

'You didn't come here to die.'

Again she dipped the fingers.

'You came here to find me,' she said.

She moistened the lips again.

'I'm not leaving till you come round.'

She heard voices outside the door. She couldn't catch the words but she sensed Grandy and the others were debating whether to come back in. The door stayed closed and the voices moved away. The fire crackled and fizzed. The storm roared on. There was no change in the woman at dusk. Hetty lay on the bed now, cradling the head, stroking the brow, her left hand holding the woman's, their fingers interlinked. The fire was the only light in the room. She'd kept it burning but it would need more turves soon. The door opened and she heard Grandy's voice.

'Time to leave it now, Hetty.'

'I'm not going.'

'You need to eat,' said Grandy. 'I'll sit with the woman. There's nothing you can do that I can't do just as well.'

'You can't make her well again.'

'Can you?'

'Yes, I can.'

Grandy walked in, stopped by the bed and looked down at the woman, then she reached out, eased Hetty's hand free and placed her own fingers over the woman's wrist.

'There's still a pulse,' said Hetty.

'I can feel it.'

'It's stronger than it was.'

'No, it isn't.'

Grandy rested the woman's hand carefully on the bed. Hetty took it again at once. Grandy watched her for a few moments, the firelight flickering over her face.

'There's no change, Hetty. She's no better than she was.'

'But she's no worse.'

'She's still dying, Hetty.'

'You're talking too loud.'

Grandy lowered her voice.

'Hetty, she's gone to a place where none of us can reach her. She's slipping away and all we can do is sit with her and give her our respect. And I can do that now. And Anna and Dolly. We can take it from here. You've done more than enough.'

'I'm not leaving till she comes round.'

'This is silly,' said Grandy. 'There are some things you can't change just by wanting.'

'This isn't just wanting.'

'It is,' said Grandy, 'and I understand it. We all want the woman to live.'

'Lorna and Gregor don't.'

'Never mind them,' said Grandy. 'All of us here want her to live. Anna does, and Dolly does, and I do. But, Hetty, sometimes you have to accept that it's a person's time to go. And I believe it's this woman's time. So get some food inside you and then have some rest. You've been here for hours and I've left you alone, but it's enough now.'

'The storm's going down,' said Hetty suddenly.

'What?' said Grandy.

'The storm's going down.'

'You're imagining that too.'

'It's definitely going down.'

Grandy leaned close.

'Listen to the noise outside, Hetty. Hear it? The wind and the sea?'

'Getting better.'

'Getting worse,' said Grandy. 'So don't say these foolish things. You can't make a storm go just by talking. And you can't make a dying woman live. Now change places with me.'

'No.'

'Do it, girl.'

'I'm not moving.'

Grandy shook her head.

'I don't know what's come over you.' She looked away, frowning. 'You've let the fire go down too.'

'I was just about to fix it when you came in.'

'Do it now, then.'

'And let you take my place?'

'I won't,' said Grandy.

'I'll do it when you've left the room.'

Grandy gave a sigh, made up the fire, and stood back, watching it blaze again.

'You've got a big heart, Hetty,' she said eventually, 'and I love you for it, but I wish you weren't so stubborn. Do you want something to drink?'

'I'll drink when the woman drinks,' said Hetty.

Grandy left the room without a word. Hetty leaned down to the woman again and cradled her head. From far below came the crash of waves as they thundered into the cliff and for a moment the island seemed as fragile as the woman lying here. Hetty drew a long breath and waited for the silence to reclaim the room; and after a while it did, falling over them like a cloak. The storm continued outside and somehow, in the contradictory peace of the room, the woman went on living.

# *Chapter 15*

Night, and still the pulse flickered, just discernible in the cold wrist. The fire burned, a small glow in the heavy darkness of the room. Hetty lay on the bed, the woman pulled close, blankets wrapped around her. It was like hugging a broken doll. Grandy came in. Hetty said nothing, but her grandmother too was silent. She had been in several times to make up the fire, sometimes with Dolly, sometimes with Anna, sometimes all three together.

They had long since stopped trying to make her leave the woman, and as the hours had passed, she had sensed the change in them. There was no disapproval in their faces now. They came and went, nursing the fire, watching, moving on, coming back; and here was Grandy again, and this time she stayed. She drew the little chair over to the fire and sat there, staring at the glowing peat.

The door opened again, and Anna and Dolly came silently in. Hetty looked up at them. Dolly squeezed her shoulder, and the two women walked over to join Grandy. There were no more chairs in the room, but neither seemed to care. They simply sat on the floor, either side of Grandy, and stared, like her, into the fire; and Hetty leaned close to the woman again, whispering as before.

'Live.'

The night moved on, the wind and the sea still loud, yet countered by the silence in the room. The women by the fire were shadows now, lit by the flicker of the flames.

Sometimes one dozed, sometimes another, but always one was awake and usually two, and as the first light of dawn started to seep through the window, Hetty sensed the alertness of all three, and their attention on her and on the woman in the bed.

She sensed other things too: a change in the note of the wind, the sound of the sea, and now people talking outside the cottage: Mackie, Isla, Tam, Lorna, Gregor, and others she couldn't make out, all waiting, no doubt, for the woman to live or die. The woman herself was as she'd been all night: cold, still, unresponsive.

Grandy struggled up from the chair, breathing heavily. Dolly and Anna stood up too, and all three walked over to the bed. They looked weary in the gathering light. Grandy rested a hand on Hetty's shoulder.

'Take a break now.'

Hetty shook her head.

'But you haven't left the bed once,' said Grandy. 'Not even to—'

'I'm staying,' said Hetty. 'I told you. I'm not leaving till she wakes up.'

'We won't take your place,' said Grandy. 'I give you my word on that. You can come straight back and be with her again. Just have some time away.'

'I'm staying.' She looked hard at Grandy. 'Please don't ask me again.'

'All right,' said Grandy, 'but I'm staying here with you.'

'Now who's being stubborn?'

Grandy glanced round at Dolly and Anna.

'We'll stay too,' said Dolly. 'I'll get you your chair, Grandy.'

'You have it,' said Grandy. She sat down on the edge of the bed. 'I'm all right here.'

'I'll find something to sit on,' said Anna.

She left the room and returned with one of the stools. Dolly drew the chair across from the fire and the two women sat down. Hetty watched them all for a moment, secretly glad that they were there, then she turned back to the woman in the bed.

'Everything's going to be all right,' she whispered.

She eased the blankets round the body, rested an arm over the woman's shoulder, leaned close to her face.

'Everything's going to be all right.'

She felt for the pulse. It was still there, but still faint. She let go of the wrist and held the woman's hand. The voices came back outside: Mackie's, and now Rory's and Hal's and Isla's. They were saying something about the wind. Then Anna spoke.

'The storm's easing,' she said.

A reluctant light was filtering into the room. The fire burned on, fed now and then by Dolly or Anna, but mostly content to be left; and the woman in the bed continued to breathe.

'Come back,' Hetty whispered to her. 'Come back.'

More light, more silence as the fury drained from wind and sea. Hetty stared down at the woman and thought of the face she had seen in the sea glass; and the faces she had never seen, though she'd looked for them every day of her life.

'Hetty,' said Grandy.

It was a kindly voice, and Hetty knew what it meant. She kept a firm hold of the woman's hand. Grandy spoke again.

'I think she's gone, Hetty. I think she's stopped breathing.'

Hetty stared at the woman's face again. It was as impassive as ever, but there was a remoteness in it that had not been there before.

'Let me check her pulse,' said Grandy.

'I'm not letting go of her hand,' said Hetty. 'You'll have to use the other wrist.'

'All right.'

Grandy felt for it among the blankets. Hetty watched, aware of Anna and Dolly waiting, as she was.

'No pulse,' said Grandy after a moment. 'I'm sorry, sweetheart.'

'You couldn't have done more, Hetty,' said Anna.

'No!' said Hetty. 'It's not right!'

She tightened her grip on the woman's hand.

'It's not right!'

Grandy touched her on the arm.

'You did well, Hetty,' she said. 'You did all you could.'

Hetty looked up at her, fighting tears.

'It counts for nothing,' she said, 'if the woman's dead.'

She stiffened suddenly.

'What is it?' said Dolly.

'She's squeezing my hand.'

The women moved quickly round the bed. Dolly took the other wrist, felt for a pulse. Grandy and Anna leaned closer. Hetty stared down. The woman's face was motionless as before, yet beneath the stillness she sensed movement, just as she'd felt it in the small hand, and was feeling it now.

'There's a pulse,' said Dolly. 'It's come back.'

'I don't believe it,' said Anna.

'She's still squeezing my hand,' said Hetty.

'I'll get some more water,' said Anna, 'and heat up some soup. We might just get some inside her.'

And she hurried from the room.

'Let's get her as warm as we can,' said Grandy. 'Hetty, you'll have to move this time. We can't tidy the bed with you lying there.'

Hetty stood up, still holding the woman's hand as Grandy and Dolly tidied the bed.

'Let go of her hand, Hetty,' said Grandy, 'just while we tuck things in that side.'

Hetty grudgingly let go. The woman's eyes opened at once, and she gave a moan.

'Easy,' said Hetty.

She took the woman's hand again. The face had suddenly come alive, the eyes moving this way and that; then they fixed on her.

'I know,' Hetty said to her. 'You're looking for me.'

She sat down on the bed, ignoring the half-tidied sheets and blankets. Grandy and Dolly stood either side of her, and a moment later Anna joined them with a glass of fresh water. The woman seemed to have no interest in the others at all.

'She needs the water,' said Hetty.

'Here.' Anna held out the glass. 'You try. She obviously trusts you. I'll get back to the soup.'

Hetty took the glass, still holding the woman's hand. The woman's eyes remained fixed upon her: dark eyes, not in any way cold, but searching—searching her.

'Let's see if you can drink,' said Hetty. 'But I'll just ease your head up first.'

'Give me the glass,' said Grandy.

Hetty handed her the glass, then slipped her right hand under the woman's back and raised her a few inches. Dolly squeezed a pillow into the gap, then a small cushion. Hetty smiled down at the woman.

'Better?'

There was no response. She moved her hand to the back of the woman's neck. The white hair, tangled though it was, still harboured a softness, and even a glow from the firelight. Hetty saw the woman's face turn towards her again.

'I'm going to help you drink,' she said.

She eased the woman's head forward, then held out her free hand and felt the glass of water nudge into it.

'Thanks, Grandy.'

She moved the glass slowly to the woman's lips.

'Now, then,' she said.

She tipped the glass, just a little. A trickle of water ran down the woman's chin.

'I don't think she swallowed any of that,' said Dolly.

'She will,' said Hetty. 'Hold the glass, can you?'

Dolly took the glass and stepped back.

'No,' said Hetty, 'don't take it away. Just hold it where it was.'

Dolly held it out, Hetty dipped a finger in, and traced the tip over the woman's lips. The mouth did not move.

'I'm going to get your lips moist,' she said to the woman. 'You don't have to do anything. Just let me get your lips moist. And when you're ready, you can lick off the water, if you want to.'

She traced more water over the lips, watching the woman's eyes all the time. Anna returned, holding a large mug.

'Smell it?' Hetty said to the woman. 'Vegetable soup. Lovely.'

To her surprise, the woman's eyes flickered in the direction of the soup.

'You understood me, didn't you?' said Hetty.

The woman's tongue licked over her moist lips. Hetty took the glass of water again, trying not to hurry in her excitement.

'Let's see if you can drink now,' she said.

She eased the woman's head forward so that the mouth touched the rim of the glass, then tipped gently; and this time she saw a tiny gulp deep in the woman's throat.

'Well done,' she said. 'Do you want some more?'

As before, the woman did not speak. But she drank the rest of the water, and most of the soup; and then she slept. Hetty watched her for another half hour, then she walked out of the room, took two bites from the bread that Grandy had left for her, and stepped out into the still morning.

# *Chapter 16*

She was desperate to be alone. She yearned for rest too, but her bedroom was not the place. She wanted air and light and the peace of an island released from storm. Grandy, Anna, and Dolly had taken over by the bedside and she felt sure the woman would sleep for a good while.

But there was no prospect of solitude yet. Gregor and Lorna were watching from the gate. She walked slowly up to them. Neither smiled. From down in the bay came the sound of hammering. She stopped in front of them.

'I wasn't screaming at nothing on the beach, Lorna,' she said. 'I was screaming at Mungo and Duffy, only you didn't see them because you didn't bother to look. You shouldn't have said what you did at the meeting.'

'And you shouldn't have been listening,' said Lorna.

Hetty shrugged. The hammering went on down in the bay. She turned to Gregor.

'You must be happy.'

'Why's that?'

'They've started building the new boat.'

'Only because I pushed them,' said Gregor. He looked at her balefully. 'Well?'

'Well what?'

'Don't play games with me, girl. What's the news about the woman?'

'She's alive,' said Hetty. 'She's come round and she's had a little soup. Isn't that wonderful?'

Gregor grunted. Lorna turned and bawled down the track.

'The woman's alive!'

A figure appeared: old Harold, struggling towards them with his stick. He fixed Lorna with his gaze.

'Alive, you said?'

'Yes,' called Lorna.

Harold's face darkened.

'I knew you'd all be pleased,' said Hetty.

And she pushed through the gate and ran off down the track. Gregor shouted after her.

'No good'll come of this.'

'Go to hell!'

She ran straight at Harold. The old man stiffened, but she swerved past him at the last moment and raced on. Round the bend she saw Sara and Ailsa and some of the women from the weaving group. They started to disperse as she drew near. Hetty called out.

'Ailsa!'

Ailsa stopped and waited. Hetty caught up with her.

'Don't tell me you want the woman to die as well.'

'I don't want anyone to die,' said Ailsa, 'but some of us are frightened.'

'Frightened of what?'

'That someone else will. Per's gone and now people are asking who's next?'

Ailsa glanced round at the other women, still walking away.

'Ailsa,' said Hetty, 'the woman's come round, the storm's gone down, Mackie's started building the new boat. That's all good, isn't it?'

Ailsa frowned.

'Mora feels different,' she said. 'That's all I know.'

And she turned away. Hetty ran down to Wolfstone Ridge, cut past High Crag and the overarching rocks that ran parallel to Scar Cliff, and headed up the western side of the island. The sky was grey with no hint of sun, chilly clouds over a chilly sea. She stopped suddenly and looked about her.

Gulls were wheeling over the lower cliffs but the sea was hardly moving, even close in, though the water was white at the base of the rocks. She sensed motion further out, yet she couldn't see it. The gulls went on circling, strangely mute. Ailsa was right, she decided. Mora did feel different. An unquiet silence had fallen over the island, and even over the sea.

She walked on, fingering the sea glass in her pocket. Around the middle point of the island she stopped again. More silence, deepening all around her. She stared at the moist grass, the rocky outcrops, the hillocks and hollows. The grey light was surrendering to a paler brightness and the silence was deepening further. She strained her ears for the reassuring wash of the sea.

It was not there. She walked on, crossing the transverse paths that nicked the surface of this part of the island. Ahead were the pastures for the sheep and goats. She cut left, towards the north-western tip of the island, the ground rising steadily. She could see the water again below her, and here, close by, was the place she wanted.

Hermit's Grotto.

She climbed down into it and stood by the little rock pile in the middle. It was too sparse and disordered to be called a cairn, but the rocks had remained in the same place all the years she could remember and, according to Grandy, all the years that anyone could remember. Grandy even insisted they hadn't been moved since the hermit first put them there, but this nugget of nonsense always came with a wink. Unlike most of the older people on Mora, Grandy didn't believe in the hermit.

Hetty wasn't sure she did either, but he was nice to talk to, whether he was real or not. She sat down by the rock pile and pulled out the sea glass. It seemed a long time since she had looked into it. She thought of the two shapes she had seen there last time and wondered whether they would still be there. She held the glass high so that it caught what light the day had managed to summon, and there they were: the two forms, once joined and now clearly separate.

'You're faces,' she murmured. 'I'm sure you're faces.'

She lowered the glass, still staring hard at it. A gull passed overhead, mewing. She glanced up, disturbed by the sound she usually liked, and the gull passed on towards the eastern shore. She looked at the shapes again.

'Who are you?' she said.

She closed the glass inside her hand, lay back on the rough grass next to the rock pile, and spoke to the hermit.

'Who are they?' she said to him.

No answer came. She lay there, peering up. The air was cold and the silence deeper than ever. The sky seemed to be locked in a kind of paralysis, the clouds stopping, or being stopped, before her eyes. She willed them to move, but they remained still. She lay there for over an hour, breathing quietly; then she sat up, the sea glass tight in her hand.

She was sure she'd heard something: a sharp sound nearby. But all was quiet. She looked about her. The scraggy grass was as still as the sky, and the dew had faded from it some time ago. She looked back over the pile of rocks.

'You made a terrible job there,' she said to the hermit, 'and you had all those years to practise building a cairn. What did you spend your time doing?'

The rocks sat before her, forlornly silent. She spoke to the hermit again.

'Maybe you just spent your days thinking,' she said. 'Maybe you lit a fire here and sat cross-legged and dreamed of eternity.'

She stood up, mindful of her loneliness.

'I wish you were here now,' she said.

She tensed suddenly. Another sound—sharp, like a click. She'd definitely heard it. Another, more muffled, but now she saw what it was: a stone rolling over the grass. The others must have hit the rocky segments and made the sharper sound. She scrambled up to the edge of the grotto and tried to see who was throwing stones at her.

Though she could guess.

No sign of anyone, but there were plenty of places to hide. She heard another sharp sound behind her, whirled round and saw a stone flying through the air. It had clearly bounced off the large boulder just down the slope, so it was easy to gauge the direction from which it had come. She caught a flash of movement among the high outcrops over to the right.

Mungo, for sure, probably Duffy, too, though she couldn't see him, and a number of other figures: two of the Hamsun boys, Nessa, Jinty, and Mungo's little brother. Probably more she couldn't see. A proper army, she thought grimly. More stones came flying over. She ducked and let them pass, then looked up again. The figures had disappeared from view. She stood up and shouted at the outcrops.

'Is that the best you've got?'

No one answered; no one appeared. She ran round the grotto, picking up all the stones she could find, then sped over to the base of the rocky hill where Mungo and the others were hiding. They were still keeping out of sight but she kept her eye on the spot where she'd last seen them and flung the first stone as hard as she could. It didn't quite reach, but it bounced off the rock just below and the sound brought Mungo's head back into view.

'What's wrong?' she shouted. 'Run out of stones, have you? Or are you worried there's not enough of you up there to deal with me?'

'Get lost, Hetty!'

'Why should I?' she yelled. 'I live here same as you.'

'We don't want you with us,' called Mungo.

'That's good,' she snapped, 'because I don't want anything to do with you either. Any of you!'

More faces appeared above and stones rained down again. None hit her, though some landed close. She watched with contempt, then threw all of hers. They too missed, but now Mungo was climbing down, his face dark with anger. The others stayed back, but he came on, not looking behind. Hetty shuddered. She'd never seen him like this before and though she was determined to stand her ground, she was frightened of what he could do.

But then he stopped, a short way from her. She watched uneasily. The rage was still visible in his face but he was now staring past her shoulder. She looked slowly round and saw Tam walking towards them. He too had stones in his hand. He didn't hurry. He almost sauntered, playing with the stones as he drew near, his eyes on Mungo all the time. He stopped next to Hetty and looked at her for the first time.

'What's going on?'

She glanced at Mungo, then up at the rocks. The others had disappeared from view again. She looked back at Mungo.

'Nothing much,' she said.

Mungo sneered at her.

'Feeling all right now, Hetty? Got your knight in shining armour to fight your battles for you?'

She said nothing. Mungo walked slowly towards them. She felt Tam brace himself, but Mungo took no notice of him and stopped in front of her.

'You ought to be getting back to Moon Cottage, Hetty,' he said. 'Your special friend might need you.'

'Shut up, Mungo,' said Tam.

Mungo threw a glance at him.

'And you should be down at the boatyard,' he said, 'helping Daddy.'

'He said he doesn't need me.'

'Because you're no good?'

'Because he's got more people than he can use,' said Tam. 'Everybody wants to help with the new boat. Even your father got off his arse and volunteered.'

Mungo clenched his fists. Tam dropped his stones and did the same. Hetty stepped between them.

'Don't,' she said.

Before either of the boys could respond, there was a shout.

'Duffy!'

It was Jinty's voice. Hetty glanced up at the outcrops again. The figures had reappeared, all staring towards the south; and now they were scrambling down the slope. Hetty turned and saw Duffy racing towards them from the other direction. Jinty and the others arrived first, but Duffy was there a moment later.

'What's going on?' said Tam.

Duffy looked round at them, panting.

'There's trouble,' he said.

# Chapter 17

'I ain't coming down,' said Gregor, 'and you can't make me.'

The boatyard was crowded, not just with Mackie and his team but with Per's old friends, and others who had heard what was happening. Hetty stood at the back next to Tam, aware of the dark glances he was still exchanging with Mungo. There was no sign of Grandy.

Gregor was sitting on the uppermost rung of the ladder that rose to the top of the big timber rack. But he was not looking at the logs that had been stacked there. He was staring down at Mackie with an air of contempt; then he spotted Hetty in the crowd.

'Ah, she's here,' he called out. 'The sea glass girl. Just in time to hear the good news.'

'Enough now, Gregor,' said Mackie.

'Enough indeed,' said Gregor.

He glanced at Harold and Lorna and his other companions, and Hetty saw a nodding of heads. The old man looked back at her and called out.

'Have they told you what they're saying, sea glass girl?'

'I don't know what you're talking about.'

'How you look like that woman?' said Gregor. 'How you got her face? Younger but the same. Everybody's noticing it.'

'Nobody's noticing it,' called Tam.

Gregor sneered at him.

'That's only because you're noticing something else in it.'

Mungo chuckled nearby. Tam glared at him.

'Come down, Gregor,' said Mackie. 'Nothing to be gained by perching up there.'

Gregor kept his eyes on Hetty.

'Have they told you the other thing, sea glass girl?'

'What's the other thing?'

She saw Duffy turn to look at her.

'The timber,' he mouthed.

'That's right, boy,' said Gregor, watching him. 'The timber. But maybe Mackie don't want us all to know about that. Maybe I got to do the talking instead. Since we ain't got Per here no more to put us straight on things.'

'There's no secret about the timber, Gregor,' said Mackie. 'We've only just discovered the problem ourselves and we'd have told everyone by the end of the day, including you. You didn't need to come sniffing round the yard checking up on us.'

'Ah, but I did, didn't I?' said Gregor. 'Otherwise who's to say what kind of a tub you and your little boys'll build us?' He gave a snort. 'And now we ain't even going to have a tub.'

A buzz of talk ran round the yard.

'Tell 'em, Mackie,' said Gregor, 'or I will.'

Mackie stepped to the foot of the ladder and turned to face the group.

'The truth, Mackie,' said Gregor, looking down.

Mackie shrugged.

'Gregor's seeing a secret that's not there,' he said. 'Like I said, we've only just discovered the problem ourselves. But it's serious, no question, and the simple fact is—the logs we've been counting on are rotten.'

Hetty heard a collective gasp.

'Not all of them,' Mackie went on. 'The ones we've been keeping an eye on here are mostly fine. But the logs we brought down from North Point are diseased. I'm not sure how it happened. Clearly somebody up that end of the island should have noticed something.'

He glanced at Mungo's father for a moment, then looked away again.

'But I should have noticed it too,' he said. 'We probably all should have. I guess none of us ever expected to lose *The Pride* the way we did and maybe we just thought that when the time came to build a new boat, there'd still be enough life in the old girl for us to use her to trade for timber if we didn't have enough.'

'And now you ain't got enough,' said Gregor. 'Stupid, Mackie, stupid.'

'So it's my fault, is it?'

'No, Mackie,' said Gregor, 'amazingly it ain't even your fault this time.'

The old man's eyes searched for Hetty again.

'We know whose fault it is, don't we, sea glass girl?'

'It's nobody's fault,' she said.

Gregor shook his head.

'Still standing up for your witchy friend? Your lookalike?'

'Shut up, Gregor!' she said.

He glared down at the faces below him.

'Ain't you all worked it out yet?' he said. 'Nothing won't never come good on Mora while that woman's alive. Per tried to tell you. I'm trying to tell you.'

'Listen, all of you,' said Mackie. 'We've had a setback, I don't deny that, but all is not lost. Rory, Karl, and I have been over every single log and we've got enough good timber to build a smaller boat, about half the size of *The Pride*—'

'Half the size?' shouted Harold. 'What damn good's a boat like that? Can you trade with it? Can you fish with it? You might as well build a raft!'

'We can get to Brinda in a boat like that,' said Mackie. 'That's all I want her for. To get to Brinda and tell them we need timber and supplies.'

Gregor gave a mocking laugh.

'And are they going to deliver all those things with winter coming on? Don't know if you've noticed, Mackie, but Brinda and the other islands don't hardly send us boats no more, even in the good weather, and once the winter storms set in, that's it. And don't even ask me how you're going to sail your little honeypot through the seas we got coming over the months ahead. It's plain stupid, Mackie, and your father would never have suggested such a thing.'

'It's the only hope we've got,' said Mackie. 'I've spoken to Rory, Karl, and the others and we're all resolved. Like I say, we've got enough good timber to build a boat that's weatherly enough to get us to Brinda and back. If we work every hour we can find, we should have her afloat before the worst of the storms kick in.'

'And what about the nice people of Brinda?' said Harold. 'Like Gregor says, even if you do make it there, are they going to send a boat back with anything? I don't think so. Why should they? So it's a voyage wasted and you'll be risking lives at the same time.'

'It's got to be done,' said Mackie. 'If we don't tell people we're in trouble, we don't even give them a chance to help us.'

Mungo's father gave a growl.

'You never spoke to me about building a smaller boat, Mackie.'

Mackie looked at him.

'I'm doing it now, Bram,' he said.

Another buzz of talk ran round the group. Hetty stared at the faces. Everyone looked frightened, she thought, even Mackie. She felt for the sea glass in her pocket and closed her hand round it. As she did so, an image of the woman's face pressed itself into her mind. It too looked frightened.

'I'm coming,' she whispered to it.

Then Gregor screamed.

'You're all crazy!'

The other voices fell silent. Hetty stared up at the old man and saw he was trembling. He spoke again, in a strange, broken voice.

'I never thought I'd see a time like this,' he said, 'never thought I'd feel ashamed of my own people.'

He gripped the sides of the ladder, pressed his feet into the nearest rung, and with something of an effort, stood up.

'Don't you see?' he went on, quivering there, his gnarled hands tight round the ladder. 'This woman's come to take away all that's good on Mora. But you're all too crazy to see it.' His eyes sought Hetty again. 'And you're the craziest of the lot, sea glass girl. And the most dangerous.'

Tears ran down the old man's face.

'What have I got to do,' he murmured, 'to make you all see?'

He closed his eyes for a moment, then suddenly opened them again, looked down at them all—and fell. Shouts broke out around the boatyard and there was a rush to the front, but no one was near enough to break the old man's fall. He landed with a jolt at the base of the ladder and rolled, groaning, across the floor. Hetty stared in horror but Mackie and the others had already crowded round and blocked Gregor from view. She turned, filled with new fears, and ran out of the boatyard. Grandy was bustling down the path towards her.

'Grandy, what's happened?'

'You first, girl.'

'Gregor's fallen off the ladder.'

'By the timber rack?'

'Yes.'

'Is he alive?'

'I don't know,' said Hetty. 'They were all crowding round him and I couldn't see. What's happened, Grandy? Something's wrong. I can tell from your face.'

Grandy took her by the hand.

'The woman's gone missing. Come on.'

# Chapter 18

They strode back up the path to the top of the cliff.

'It's my fault,' said Grandy, breathing hard. 'I was on my own with her, but I didn't think she had the strength to move by herself, and she was sleeping soundly too. So I took a break by the bedside, well, a doze, and when I woke up, she was gone. I've no idea where she is.'

Hetty let go of her grandmother's hand.

'We must find her,' she said, and she raced off up the path.

'Wait,' called Grandy.

'Catch up with me at Moon Cottage.'

'Hetty, wait . . . just a minute.'

Hetty stopped.

'Hetty, listen,' said Grandy. 'Before you run off, there's something you need to know about the woman. Anna, Dolly, and I are convinced she's not in her wits. We've all tried to communicate with her, but it's hard to get any sense from her, and hard even to know if she understands anything. She's like Gilda was in her last days. You remember Gilda? You're just old enough.'

'I remember her.'

'Well, this woman's the same,' said Grandy. 'So if you do find her, don't be upset if you don't get a response. That's all I'm saying. Now run home and see if you can find her. I'll get there as fast as I can.'

Hetty sprinted back to Moon Cottage, but there was no sign of the woman, either inside or nearby. Grandy arrived, limping painfully.

'Any luck, girl?'

Hetty shook her head.

'I'm going to climb High Crag,' she said. 'I might see her from up there.'

But the summit revealed no clue as to the woman's whereabouts. Hetty peered over the familiar landscape, searching hard. Sheep and goats moved upon it, and figures she recognized, but there was no sign of the woman. She scrambled down again and ran towards the southern cliffs. She'd been avoiding this but there was nothing else for it. As the cliffs nearest to Moon Cottage, they were the most obvious danger point for the woman.

She reached Wolfstone Ridge and cut past the huge, conical boulders down to the edge. She hated this spot but she knew it would give her the best view down to the rocks below. She dropped to her knees and crawled the last few inches, then craned over and peered down. The cliff-face stretched before her, curving slightly towards the bay. No figure was visible on the rocks below. She drew a long, deep breath.

Then something touched her shoulder.

She screamed and started to pull back from the edge. The thing touched her a second time. She screamed again and twisted her head round, only to find herself staring at the woman, also on her knees. She had an arm out-stretched, and now she touched Hetty again.

'What are you doing here?' said Hetty.

The woman was still in her night clothes, and her eyes were wild and strange. Hetty crawled closer to her.

'We've been looking everywhere for you,' she said. 'Grandy and me, we've . . . '

She stopped, aware of something else in the woman's eyes.

'You were looking for me, weren't you?' she said.

The woman didn't speak.

'You were looking for me,' said Hetty, 'just like I was looking for you.'

The woman went on staring at her.

'Come on,' said Hetty. 'I'm going to carry you back to Moon Cottage. If you're not too heavy.'

She picked the woman up without difficulty.

'You're so light,' she said. 'You're like a little child.'

There was something childlike about the woman's face too, Hetty decided: childlike and ancient at the same time.

'Let's get you home,' she said.

She set off towards Wolfstone Ridge, then paused.

'Only it's not your home, is it?'

She looked into the woman's face.

'Your home is Haga. All those miles away.'

She walked on, aware once again of the silence pressing upon the island. Anna and Dolly had returned to Moon Cottage and they hurried out with Grandy to meet her.

'What's the news about Gregor?' said Hetty.

'He's alive but he's badly injured,' said Anna. 'Lorna's nursing him at her cottage, and Dolly and I are going to look in when we can. But Lorna's got other people help-ing too, so we came back here. What about this poor woman? Where did you find her?'

'By the southern cliffs.'

Dolly shook her head.

'Is she hurt?'

'I don't think so,' said Hetty. 'She's fallen asleep in my arms.'

The three women glanced at each other.

'What does that look mean?' said Hetty.

'Just that she's different with you,' said Dolly.

'She's been really difficult with the three of us,' said Anna. 'No matter how gentle we try to be, we still frighten her. But you don't, it seems.'

'And when you're not there, Hetty,' said Dolly, 'her eyes keep darting all over the place, like she's—'

'Looking for me.' Hetty glanced down at the woman's face. 'I know.'

'Has she spoken?' said Dolly.

'Not a word,' said Hetty. She looked up at Grandy. 'But you're wrong about what you said.'

'What do you mean?'

'About her not being in her wits.'

Again the three women exchanged glances.

'You did it again,' said Hetty. 'That look.'

'What are you trying to say?' said Grandy.

'She's lost some of her wits,' said Hetty, 'but she hasn't lost all of them.'

'How do you know?'

'Because she remembers me.'

'Your face at the bedside last night,' said Grandy. 'All right, she's got a picture of that in her head, and—'

'I don't mean my face at the bedside.'

'What do you mean?'

'I don't know,' said Hetty. 'I'm just telling you she remembers me.'

The woman's eyes opened again.

'Come on,' Hetty said to her. 'I'm going to wash you.'

And she started towards the cottage. The others hurried after her.

'I don't think washing her's a good idea,' said Grandy. 'The three of us tried that earlier but she got very aggressive and we had to give up.'

'She'll be all right with me,' said Hetty.

She entered the cottage and carried the woman through to the bathroom.

'Grandy?' she said.

'I know,' said Grandy. 'Hot water.'

'I'm going to wash you,' Hetty said to the woman. 'You've got a bit dirty. I'm going to make you clean again. There's nothing to be frightened of.'

The woman didn't seem frightened at all. She let Hetty sit her down, stroke her hand, undress her. Grandy and the others stayed outside and Hetty was glad of it. She felt sure the woman would dislike being seen naked by too many people.

But she was wrong. When the door opened and Grandy brought in the first jug of hot water, the woman didn't even glance in that direction. Her eyes remained fixed on Hetty's face. Hetty smoothed the sponge over the wrinkled skin.

'So what's your name?' she said softly.

No answer came.

'My name's Hetty,' she said. 'Do you want to tell me yours? I'd love to know what it is.'

Again, no answer.

Hetty smiled at the tiny face looking up at her, then glanced round. Grandy, Anna, and Dolly were all standing there.

'Can you bring some more hot water, please?' she said. 'I want to wash her hair.'

They brought more water, moving quietly without talking, and Hetty washed the woman's hair, and the whole of her body, and then dried her and dressed her in new night clothes, and carried her back to the bedroom, and helped her into bed.

'Do you want something to eat or drink?' she said.

But the woman's eyes had closed and she slept through the rest of the afternoon. At dusk she woke and looked into Hetty's face again, and then slept on. Darkness drew in. Dolly and Anna went off to see Gregor. Hetty ate what supper she could manage, then sat with Grandy by the fire. Late in the evening she heard some of the men walking home from the boatyard, then an hour later new voices, further off. She stood up, walked over to the window nearest the track, and looked out. Figures were standing on the far slopes, waiting in the darkness. She recognized Harold among them.

'They want the woman dead, Grandy,' she murmured.

She watched them for a while, then frowned.

And maybe they want me dead too, she thought.

# Chapter 19

Grandy joined her by the window and stared out at the figures in the night.

'Why are they so superstitious?' said Hetty.

'They'd say you're superstitious,' said Grandy, 'with all your sea glass talk.'

'You haven't answered my question.'

'They just are,' said Grandy. 'It's no different on the other islands. The ones I've been to anyway. There are people there just like Per and Gregor.'

'They frighten me,' said Hetty.

'You've never acted like they frighten you,' said Grandy. 'You've always been spirited, like your mother was. You've stood up for yourself with Per, and done the same with Gregor.'

'They still always frightened me,' said Hetty, 'and Grandy . . . I keep seeing Gregor standing on the ladder. It was like—'

'I know,' said Grandy. 'Anna told me what others are saying, people who were there. It's like no one's sure if he lost his balance or his footing or—'

'If he jumped,' said Hetty.

'Yes.' Grandy looked round at her. 'What do you think?'

Hetty pictured the old man's face, as he stood atop the ladder.

'I think . . . I've become scared of Mora,' she said, and she could add no more.

Grandy returned to the fire, worked it a little with the poker, and sat down again. Hetty watched her for a while, then turned back to the window. Most of the figures were moving off now, but some still lingered on the high ground by Wolfstone Ridge.

'Come and sit down,' said Grandy.

'I'll just make sure the woman's all right.'

'She's fine.'

'I'll check anyway.'

The woman was sleeping, but her face looked gaunt. Hetty made her way back to the main room and sat down again.

'Grandy?'

'Mm?'

'I so want the woman to live.'

'I know you do, sweetheart,' said Grandy, 'and so do I, but she's not going to make it, I'm afraid. I know you don't want me to talk this way, but I can't lie to you. You revived her, and that was very well done, but it's only going to be for a short while. We've fed her and washed her and done all we can, and she's shown incredible resilience, far more than you'd expect from someone so old and frail. But she must be near her end now.'

'I wish Lorna and the others didn't hate her so much.'

'They're frightened,' said Grandy, 'just like you are.'

'Why?'

'People scare easily on Mora.'

'But—'

'I know,' said Grandy. 'You're going to tell me the people of Mora are brave, and you'd be right. They always have been. They've got no choice. Tiny little island like this, miles from anywhere, rough seas all around us. It's no wonder we get so few boats calling. So yes, the people of Mora are very brave. It's the isolation that gives them their courage.'

'So what do you mean when you say they scare easily?'

'I'm talking about a different kind of fear.'

'And where does that come from?'

'Same place,' said Grandy. 'The isolation.'

'I don't understand, Grandy.'

'I'm not sure I do either, girl,' said Grandy, poking the fire again.

Hetty stood up again and walked back to the window. All the figures were gone now.

'I'm going to sit with the woman for a bit,' said Grandy.

'I'll come with you.'

'No, Hetty, go to bed.'

'I'm coming with you.'

Grandy shook her head.

'You're so stubborn, Hetty.'

'You keep telling me.'

'Because you keep being stubborn.'

'I get it from you,' said Hetty.

'You get it from your mother.'

'And she got it from you.'

'True,' said Grandy.

They entered the spare room. The woman was still asleep and showed no sign of waking. Hetty studied the face again. In spite of the gauntness, it still had that child-like quality she had seen earlier. The breathing was quiet and slow, but every so often it seemed to hesitate. A tiny figure, Hetty thought: almost a fragment of a human being.

'Get some rest, Hetty,' said Grandy. 'It's my shift.'

'I'll change with you in a couple of hours.'

'No, you won't,' said Grandy. 'You were with her all last night. It's my turn now.'

'Not for the whole night.'

'Yes, for the whole night,' said Grandy. 'Go to bed. I'll wake you in the morning.'

'But—'

'I promise I'll call you if there's anything.'

Hetty leaned over the bed, staring at the still face of the woman.

'Enough now,' said Grandy.

'All right.'

She peered at Grandy in the shadowy light of the room. There was nothing childlike about her grandmother's face.

'Goodnight, Grandy.'

'Goodnight, Hetty.'

She stepped out of the room, closed the door behind her, and stood there, the image of the woman strong in her mind, and with it a powerful urge to go back in. Yet she knew Grandy would only send her out again, and she was now desperately tired. She walked over to the window by the track and peered out once more. The figures had not returned to Wolfstone Ridge.

She made her way through to her bedroom and closed the door behind her. All was still within the small, familiar space, but she could feel a tension in the silence, and in herself. She stood there for several minutes, her mind on the woman again, and that hesitant respiration; then she stepped up to the window and stared over the sea. It was glistening under the moon, barely a wave visible.

She pushed open the window and let a breath of cool air float in, and with it came the whispers from the sea. A flicker of wind ruffled her face. She reached into her pocket, pulled out the sea glass and framed it against the moon, and the glow pushed through it, clearly showing the shapes she'd seen before: the two images, so like faces, yet hard to make out.

Sleep was creeping over her. She placed the sea glass on the table and changed into her night clothes. A sudden chill made her shiver. She put her dressing gown on too, slipped the sea glass into a pocket, and climbed into bed. The sea went on whispering below. She closed her eyes and lay back. The night moved on and some part of her mind moved with it, dreaming of the woman in the spare room, and the faces she'd seen in the sea glass, and those she had looked for but never found.

Then at some point she was wide awake and on her feet again. She wasn't sure what had prompted her to rise. The room seemed darker than before. She walked to the window and saw that the moon had vanished behind cloud cover, and the sea was a murky grey, its surface moving eerily in the night. She slipped out and crept down to the spare room. The door was open and Grandy was asleep in the chair.

The bed was empty.

She looked frantically about her. There was no sign of the woman anywhere. She opened her mouth to call to Grandy, then changed her mind and ran softly through to the main room. The front door was open. She raced out into the night and stopped on the path. The woman was over by the rocks where the high ground fell away to the bay. She was whirling about, her arms flailing.

'I'm here,' called Hetty.

The woman turned, saw her, and came stumbling across in what was clearly meant to be a run, but she had no balance and she tumbled to the ground. Hetty rushed over to her and bent down.

'It's all right,' she said, 'it's all right.'

The woman was moaning and reaching for her.

'I've got you,' said Hetty, pulling her close.

The woman was whimpering now, but she seemed less agitated already, and she did not appear to have broken any bones in the fall.

135

'You were searching for me again, weren't you?' said Hetty. 'You woke up and found I wasn't there, so you went looking for me. I wish you'd come to my room and not out here.'

She glanced towards the edge of the high ground, with its fatal drop beyond.

'Come on,' she said. 'I'll carry you back into the cottage.'

She bent down to pick the woman up, then felt a hand tugging at her wrist. She stopped and looked down. The woman was staring towards the rocks at the edge of the high ground overlooking the bay.

'You want to go over to the rocks?' said Hetty.

There was no answer.

'Or is it the sea?' she said. 'Is that what you're interested in?'

As she spoke, she felt the whispers again from far below. She picked the woman up and carried her towards the rocks. Beyond them the ground dropped away, first to the path that cut down to the bay, then to the sloping ground that fell to the shingle beach. She stopped by the first of the rocks, keeping well back from the edge. The woman's eyes were fixed on the sea.

'What are you looking for?' said Hetty.

The woman turned and stared at her.

'You understood me, didn't you?' said Hetty. 'You understood what I just asked you. Even if you can't answer.'

The woman turned back to the sea.

'We'll go closer,' said Hetty, 'but only a bit.'

She walked as far as the long, flat rock at the far end.

'Let's sit here for a while.'

She placed the small figure carefully on the rock, then slipped off her dressing gown and draped it round the woman's shoulders so that she sat there like a tiny ghost.

'That's better,' said Hetty.

She sat down too and put an arm round the woman's shoulder.

'Grandy and I often sit here,' she said. 'It's a good place to watch the sea.'

'Whispers,' said the woman suddenly.

'What did you say?' said Hetty.

The woman did not speak again, but went on staring over the sea. Hetty listened to the sounds from the water, the soft sounds that seemed to reach up from far below the surface. She let her free hand slip into the pocket of the dressing gown, then pulled out the sea glass and held it up to the sky.

'Can you see?' she said to the woman.

She wasn't sure what she was asking. The shapes in the glass were hidden now, but the moon was still covered and all was dark. She searched the sea for something bright to hold the glass against, but there was nothing: just the grey-black water, strangely still. She brought the sea glass closer to their faces, then glanced at the woman. She was peering past the sea glass at the water and seemed to have no interest in it at all. Hetty lowered her arm, keeping the glass in her open palm. The woman's eyes dropped, then she touched the sea glass with a finger, hesitantly, as though it might scald her.

'Here,' said Hetty.

She held it out. The woman did not take it.

'It's sea glass,' said Hetty. 'It's from out there.'

She glanced towards the water, then back again. The woman was still peering down at the glass.

'You can't see it very clearly,' said Hetty.

She held it higher, wishing there were more light, but suddenly, in spite of the cloudy dark, the images came back: the two mysterious shapes. She studied them, wondering

137

whether the woman would be like everybody else, and not see. The woman took the sea glass from her, folded it in her hand, and spoke again.

'Whispers.'

Hetty watched her, unsure what to think; then she heard the sound of running steps. She turned towards the cottage and saw Tam racing up the path to the door, clearly unaware of them. He knocked loudly, and then again.

'Tam,' she called.

He looked round and saw them.

'What's going on?' she said.

Before he could answer, the door of the cottage opened and Grandy appeared.

'What's happened?' she said.

Tam looked from one to the other, then turned to Hetty.

'Father sent me ahead to warn you in case there's trouble.'

He paused.

'Gregor's died.'

# Chapter 20

More figures appeared on the track: Lorna, Mungo's father, and old Harold, thrusting his stick into the ground as he drove himself to keep up. Hetty saw the woman watching them fearfully. Grandy called across.

'Hetty, bring her inside!'

She picked up the woman and hurried towards the cottage, but Lorna and the others had left the track now and were halfway down the path to the door. Grandy bustled forward and stood in front of them.

'That's far enough,' she said. 'You don't want to do something you'll regret.'

'We ain't going to do nothing we'll regret,' said Harold.

But they stopped. Tam ran up to Grandy and stood beside her.

'You mustn't hurt the woman,' he said.

'Keep out of it, boy,' said Harold.

'I'm not a boy,' said Tam.

But the old man wasn't listening.

'We've lost two men now, Grandy,' he said. 'Two good men in about as many days, both of them old friends I grew up with. And we've lost *The Pride*.' He pointed his stick at the woman in Hetty's arms. 'And everything was fine till that witch turned up.'

'So what are you going to do?' said Hetty. 'Kill her?'

'We don't have to kill her,' said Harold, 'and neither do you. All you got to do is stop feeding her and she'll die by herself.'

'Hear, hear,' said Lorna, and Mungo's father grunted his agreement.

'I can't believe you can say that,' said Grandy, 'or even think it.'

'I can,' said Hetty. She stared at the three angry faces, hating them. 'And how's letting this woman die going to make anything better?' she said. 'Is it going to bring Per back? Or Gregor?'

'It won't bring them back,' said Lorna, 'but it'll be fair and it'll be right.'

'Exactly,' said Harold.

'But she's done nothing wrong,' said Hetty.

'She's a jinx,' said Harold. 'Per was right, Gregor was right. She's brought nothing but evil to this island and she'll bring more if we let her live.'

He took a step closer to Hetty.

'Keep back,' said Hetty, pulling the woman into her chest.

'I ain't going to hurt her,' said the old man. 'I wouldn't demean myself.'

He walked slowly forward and peered down at the woman in Hetty's arms. Hetty kept her eyes on his stick. But Harold didn't use his stick. He simply spat.

'You bastard,' said Hetty.

She turned her back to him and wiped the spittle from the woman's cheek with her sleeve. Behind her she heard Grandy berating the old man, then, to her relief, she saw Mackie striding up the path.

'Bit late for a meeting,' he said.

'We've got business,' said Lorna.

'I don't think you have,' said Mackie. 'You should be at your homes.'

He threw a glance at Mungo's father.

'Especially you, Bram. Early start tomorrow. We want to get a good day's work behind us at the boatyard before Gregor's burial service in the evening.'

'I won't be at the boatyard,' said Bram. 'I'll be tending my stock.'

'And I won't be at Gregor's service,' said Hetty.

'You ain't invited to the service,' said Harold, 'because you wasn't no friend of Gregor, nor Per, and you ain't no friend of Mora neither.'

'Enough of that,' said Mackie. He looked at Mungo's father again. 'So you're not coming to the boatyard tomorrow?'

'Like I said, I'll be tending my stock.'

'Suit yourself, Bram. Plenty more where you came from.'

'I don't think so.'

'Oh, I do,' said Mackie. He put an arm round Tam's shoulder. 'My boy can take your place and do just as well, I'm sure, if not better.'

'Hetty,' said Grandy, 'get the woman to bed.'

'Sound advice,' said Mackie.

'Do you want some help, Hetty?' said Tam.

'I can manage.'

Hetty caught Grandy's eye, then looked again at Tam.

'You could check the fire in the spare room,' she said.

Tam disappeared inside the cottage. Hetty turned back to Lorna and her companions.

'This woman's come through a terrible storm in a tiny boat,' she said. 'She's from Haga but she probably doesn't remember that because she's confused and frightened, but she's clinging on to life somehow, and all you want to do is blame her for everything that's gone wrong here, and then let her die. You're heartless!'

'And you're young,' said Harold. 'If you'd lived as long as we have, you'd understand better. You'd know where evil comes from.'

'That's right,' said Lorna.

'I'm as old as both of you, near enough,' said Grandy, 'and I'll tell you where evil comes from. It comes from ignorance and bitterness and empty hearts.'

'That crone's caused nothing but sorrow,' said Lorna. 'She should be left to die.'

'We won't do that,' said Grandy.

'Then you can expect no more help from this community,' said Lorna. 'Count on that, Grandy. Because I'm telling you, everyone on Mora thinks like we do.' She turned to Harold and Bram. 'Let's go.'

And the three of them set off down the path.

'Hot air,' said Mackie, as they disappeared from view. 'You've got plenty of friends on Mora.'

Tam reappeared in the doorway.

'The fire's going in the spare room,' he said. 'I checked the main fire too.'

'Thank you, Tam,' said Grandy.

Hetty saw Tam look at her.

'Thank you, Tam,' she managed.

Mackie put an arm round his son's shoulder again.

'We'll be off, Grandy,' he said, 'but listen, any more trouble and you send Hetty to fetch me.'

'Us,' said Tam.

'That's right,' said Mackie. 'Send her to fetch us.'

'Thank you,' said Grandy.

And Mackie and Tam were gone.

'Come on, Hetty,' said Grandy. 'Let's go in.'

They closed the door behind them and Hetty carried the woman towards the fire. Its glow lit the fear that continued to haunt the withered face. Grandy leaned closer and the woman started to whimper.

'You're frightening her, Grandy,' said Hetty.

'I know.' Grandy leaned back. 'Just as well she's not scared of you.'

'I'm going to put her back in the bed.'

'Probably best, though I don't suppose she'll sleep.'

'I'm going to get in with her.'

'Are you sure?' said Grandy. 'I can sit with her if you like. She doesn't seem to mind that so much. It's only when I'm close to her.'

'I want to do it, Grandy.'

They made their way through to the spare room. Grandy pulled back the blankets and sheet, Hetty laid the woman carefully down, and then climbed in with her. The woman cast a wary glance towards Grandy as she tidied the bedclothes around them.

'I'll leave you for a bit,' said Grandy, straightening up, 'but I'll look in at some point and see how you are. If you need a break and a proper sleep in your own bed, come and get me and I'll sit in the chair and keep an eye on her.'

'All right.'

Grandy left the room and Hetty slipped an arm round the woman. There was no resistance but as she pulled the thin body closer, she felt something chafe against her arm. She looked down and, to her surprise, saw the sea glass clasped in the woman's left hand. She stared. It was hard to believe she hadn't noticed it there all this time, or that the woman hadn't dropped it. She gently took the sea glass from her and held it up.

'You like this, don't you?' she said.

The woman stared at it, then at her.

'It's from the ocean,' said Hetty. 'It's been smoothed and shaped by the water.'

She held it out in front of them, so that the glow from the fire in the corner of the room played through the glass, and there were the two images she had seen before; and suddenly they were clearer than they had ever been. They were unquestionably faces now. The one on the right was a girl. Hetty frowned. The face looked a little like hers, but perhaps this was fanciful, she thought. The other face looked like an ancient man. The woman reached out and stroked the glass with her thumb.

'Can you see the faces?' said Hetty. She hesitated. 'Do you . . . do you know who they are?'

The woman turned towards her, trembling.

'Easy now,' said Hetty.

She placed the sea glass on the bedside table, then pulled the woman close again, and after a while the trembling stopped, and the woman fell asleep. Outside the room, all was quiet, and it was clear that Grandy had gone to bed. Hetty lay there, staring up at the ceiling and fretting once more about all that had happened, and what the future might hold. Whatever it was, she sensed it must be dark. The whispers from the sea started again.

She listened to them. They were soft and delicate and broken by small silences, as though the sea were gathering breath; and in those pauses she held her own, as she waited for the whispers to return, which they did. It was consoling to hear them: there seemed so few constancies left now. She turned her head to the side. The woman was still sleeping. She looked the other way and saw the sea glass resting on the bedside table.

Another mystery too deep to solve. She gave a long sigh and pondered her solitude. She'd always embraced it

144

here on Mora, but now that cloistered strength felt threatened. She pictured her father and mother, or rather the fantasy father and fantasy mother she always saw when she thought of them, based on the descriptions Grandy had given her. The mental images were clear in her mind, but they were nothing like the faces she'd seen down the years in pieces of sea glass like this one.

She wondered for the thousandth time who those other faces were. The woman lying next to her was the only person who had ever emerged from the frozen image into real life. The other faces were like vapour. She'd always assumed they were the dead—so many people had drowned in the ghost water of Mora over the centuries—but recently she'd started to question this. The sea had changed in the last few years, and the whispers had changed too; and now the sea glass had given her two more images: a girl who looked like her and an ancient man.

Still more mysteries. There seemed no answer to anything right now. The whispers fell silent, the night moved on, the woman continued to sleep. Hetty lay there, on the edge of tears; and then suddenly the idea came. It was so wild and so dangerous she pushed it away at once, but it fought back, driving itself into her mind until finally it mastered her and she gave it her attention. She closed her eyes and tried to take in all that it meant. Everything about the idea was frightening, except for one thing: the possibility that it might just work. The burden of that possibility pressed itself upon her as she drifted into sleep.

# Chapter 21

Daybreak and the burden was still there; but she had woken with her mind made up. She lay there, thinking hard and trying not to flinch from what was to come. She turned her head to the side. The woman was curled up in the crook of her arm, still asleep. The breaths were quiet, almost inaudible, not panicky as they had been last night; fragile, however.

Light was pushing into the room and gulls were mewing over the western cliffs. Hetty listened to them for a while, trying also to catch the conversation of the waves, but the sounds of the sea were too subtle, her mood too distracted. She went through everything in her mind again. There was so much to do, so much to get right, and one of the things was to see Tam. She had to see Tam.

Grandy appeared in the doorway.

'Have you slept, Hetty?'

'Not much.'

'Nor me.'

Grandy glanced at the woman.

'Least somebody's getting some rest.'

'She needs it more than we do.'

'Speak for yourself.'

Grandy slumped in the chair, breathing heavily.

'Take a break, Hetty,' she said. 'I'll watch her for a bit.'

Hetty crept out of the room, washed, dressed and slipped out of the cottage. The light was growing fast and the sea was bright and still. A pale sun was climbing over the horizon and there was a sharp chill in the air. She stood there, staring down into the bay where small waves were breaking on the shingle beach. She thought of Tam again, but then Grandy called through the window.

'The woman's woken up.'

They washed and fed her, and helped her back to bed when she was too tired to sit by the fire, and soon she was sleeping on. It seemed all she wanted to do now. From down in the boatyard came the sounds of sawing and hammering. Yet again Hetty thought of Tam and she was on the point of trying to think of an excuse to go and find him when, to her relief, he knocked at the door.

'Come in, Tam,' said Grandy.

He walked into the main room and stood there in front of them, glancing towards the window.

'I thought you were helping your father at the boat-yard,' said Grandy.

'I was,' he said, still looking away. 'I mean, I am. But he said I could come and see you for a few minutes.'

Grandy's eyes sparkled for a moment.

'That was kind of him,' she said. 'So what can we do for you?'

'I just came to see if you're both all right.'

'Hetty's fine, thanks.'

'Oh, but . . . ' Tam looked quickly round. 'I meant you too, Grandy.'

Grandy laughed, then suddenly frowned and leaned forward.

'What have you done to your face, Tam?'

'Nothing.'

'Are you trying to hide a bruise?'

Tam shot a glance at Hetty.

'Keep still,' said Grandy. She felt round his temple. 'Hm, you are trying to hide a bruise. Bit ugly but you'll probably survive.' She looked him over. 'Tell Hetty about it while I go and see how our guest's getting on.'

'She's sleeping,' said Hetty.

'I'll check anyway,' said Grandy, and she disappeared.

Hetty and Tam looked at each other.

'What happened to you?' she said.

'Can we go outside?'

'All right.'

They stepped out of the cottage and wandered over to the long flat stone. Below them the water in the bay was still calm but a breeze from the north-east was starting to ripple the sea beyond.

'Do you want to sit down?' said Tam.

'Let's stand.'

'All right.'

'What happened to you?' she said.

'I got hit.'

'Who by?'

'Mungo,' said Tam, 'but don't worry. He came off worse.'

Hetty studied the bruise. It was as Grandy had said: ugly but not serious.

'What were you fighting about?' she said.

'You.'

'Me?'

'Yeah,' said Tam. 'It was early this morning. Mungo was mouthing all this horrible stuff about you. I told him to shut up and he wouldn't. So we had a fight. And then Duffy pitched in. I didn't expect that.'

'He'll always stick up for Mungo.'

'He wasn't sticking up for Mungo,' said Tam. 'He was sticking up for me. Well, you.'

'Duffy was?'

'Yeah, I think he's had enough of Mungo.'

'So what happened?'

'Father came and separated us and sent us all off in different directions. Hetty, listen.' Tam paused. 'Lorna and the others were wrong last night. You mustn't believe them. It's not everyone on the island against you. It's just some. My father and mother aren't against you, and neither are Anna or Dolly, or Ailsa or Sara, or most of the men at the boatyard, like Hal and Karl and Rory. They're all on our side.'

'Our side?'

Hetty turned away and stared over the sea.

'There never used to be sides on Mora,' she said.

'Well, there are now.'

She thought again of the decision she had made; and she thought again of Tam. But he spoke first.

'Hetty?'

She turned back to him and saw the fear in his face.

Fear of her.

'You seem strange,' he said.

'Do I?'

'Kind of like . . . you're here and you're not here.'

'I am here, Tam,' she said. 'I promise I'm here.'

But she knew she was lying to him again. She tried to remember the truth, the thing she knew she had to say. She stared down at the ground.

'I'm glad you're on my side, Tam,' she said. 'I really . . . '

She looked up at him again.

'I really value your friendship. I just want you to know that.'

She leaned forward and kissed him softly on the mouth, then started to pull back. He drew her swiftly close again and kissed her deeply, and she let him, and kissed him

149

back in turn, and then she stepped apart, frightened of the pain she knew she was going to cause him. It was in his face already and she hated herself for putting it there.

'Hetty—' he began.

'Don't.'

'Don't what?'

'Don't say it.'

He looked at her, breathing hard.

'I must go back in,' she said, 'and you must get back to the boatyard.'

They stood there, staring at each other, then Tam shifted on his feet.

'All right,' he said.

But neither of them moved. She touched him on the arm.

'Take care of yourself, Tam.'

'I'll see you, Hetty.'

'Take care of yourself, all right?'

She turned and hurried towards the cottage, hoping he wouldn't see the tears breaking out; but he didn't call after her and when she reached the door and looked round again, he was through the gate and running away down the track. He didn't look over his shoulder. She watched him disappear from view, then wiped her eyes and turned to the door, trying to collect herself; but it swung open at that moment and there was Grandy looking out.

'Time to eat, Hetty,' she said briskly. 'I've made some porridge and I've got some fresh eggs from Anna and I'm going to get some food down you if it's the last thing I do. And down the woman too, with any luck.'

Somehow Grandy managed both. The day wore on. Grandy busied herself at the spinning wheel and the woman slept again, and Hetty was glad of it. She needed time to prepare herself, to be alone with her thoughts. She slipped out to High Crag and climbed to the top and stood there for a while, looking down over the island, then, as light started to fail, she ran back to Moon Cottage, checked all was well with the woman and with Grandy, and then walked through to her room and sat on the bed, and stared round at all the old familiar things. Then she stepped up to the window and gazed over the sea.

Dusk was only a short way off and she could feel its frown upon the water. Outside she heard some of the men returning early from the boatyard to make ready for Gregor's burial service in the chapel. She could hear Grandy too in the next room, brushing down her best clothes. She eased her gaze towards the horizon. Far beyond it to the south were the other islands of the archipelago, places she'd never wanted to see. She knew about them from what others had told her, but they were as insubstantial to her as dreams.

She pictured Brinda, the island Mackie hoped to reach when the small new boat was built, and wondered for a moment whether there was a fifteen-year-old girl like her there staring into the dusk-heavy sea just as she was right now, perhaps even looking this way. She peered over the water, straining for the far distance, but the dusk was thickening as evening ghosted the corners of the sea. She went on hugging the horizon with her eyes, but it was no good. Everything was turning grey and blackness was close behind. She heard Grandy's voice outside her room.

'I'm going now, Hetty.'

She stepped quickly out.

'You look very nice, Grandy.'

'I look very silly,' said Grandy. 'I always do in my best clothes. But it's kind of you to pretend otherwise. You'll be all right with the woman?'

'Yes.'

'I'll be some time. You know how these things are.'

'Are you nervous about going?' said Hetty. 'With Lorna and some of the others being so unfriendly?'

'I'm not bothered about them at all,' said Grandy, 'and neither should you be. Hold your head up, girl, and follow your conscience in all things. If you do that, you'll never need to worry about small minds.'

Hetty looked down.

'You all right?' said Grandy.

'Fine.' She looked quickly up again. 'I'm fine.'

'Are you sure?' said Grandy. 'I don't have to go. Gregor wouldn't want me at his burial anyway. He'd much rather be at mine.'

'No, you must go,' said Hetty. 'You really must.'

She kissed Grandy hurriedly on the cheek, and then again. Grandy frowned.

'You don't normally do that.'

'Do what?'

'Kiss me.'

'I've kissed you lots of times.'

'Not that way.'

'I'm fine, Grandy, really.'

Grandy went on watching her, then slowly turned away.

'I'll see you later, Hetty,' she said.

And she walked towards the front door. Hetty watched her go, fighting the urge to say something more. Somehow she remained silent and Grandy stepped outside, and was gone. A heavy stillness fell upon the cottage. Hetty stood there, struggling with tears again, but somehow she calmed herself and walked through to the spare room. The woman was still asleep.

'Don't wake,' Hetty whispered, and she closed the door again.

It took far longer than she'd expected to gather all the things, and at every turn she feared detection, but everyone, it seemed, had gone to the chapel and she met nobody on her trips to and from the bay. At last she had everything ready and there was just one more thing to do: the note to Grandy. She wrote it carefully, in her very best handwriting, and put it on the table by the fire, then she picked up the heavy clothes she'd collected and carried them through to the spare room. The woman opened her eyes as she entered: as though she'd been waiting.

'You know, don't you?' said Hetty.

The woman watched her sleepily; then Hetty saw that the left hand was closed in a fist.

'You're holding the sea glass again,' she said.

She could see the edge protruding.

'I'm going to dress you,' she said.

The woman did not resist or even take notice as Hetty slipped on the thick clothes that she'd taken from her wardrobe. It was as well that the two of them were a similar size, though the woman was so gaunt that the clothes still seemed to smother her. But at least she would be as warm as possible with the pullovers, jacket, and woollen hat. Hetty pulled on her own heavy clothes, then—with some difficulty now they were both so weighed down— she picked up the woman and carried her outside.

The water below was calm, the wind light and still from the north-east, but the sky was dark with clouds covering the moon and stars. She carried the woman to the edge of the high ground, and stood there with her, staring down. The sea moved like a shadow and doubts filled her again. Within a few hours, she thought, perhaps even a few minutes, they could both be dead.

She glanced over her shoulder at Moon Cottage. It too was dark, but something flickered in the nearest window.

She stared at it, searching for Grandy's face, wanting it almost, but no one was there. It was just the remnant glow of the fire, struggling to stay alive. She took a long look at the cottage, then pulled the woman closer and set off down the path to the bay. The water below them was silent and black with just a thin line of phosphorescence where the surf nibbled at the shore. Hetty nodded down to the shingle beach.

'There she is,' she said, 'my little dinghy. I've moved her closer to the water and stepped the mast and stowed all the things we need in her. Can you see her? She's called *Baby Dolphin* and I've had her since I was ten. Mackie built her for me.'

The woman said nothing, nor did she look at the boat. She had tucked her head back and she was staring up at the sky.

'All cloudy tonight,' said Hetty. 'Nothing to see up there.'

'Stars,' said the woman.

Hetty stopped and peered up at the sky, but there were no stars to be seen. She looked back at *Baby Dolphin* and shuddered for a moment. There was no question that Mackie had built her well. She was easy to row and easy to sail with her single lugsail, but she had never been more than half a mile from Mora, never had to face rough weather, and there was barely room in her for the two of them, let alone the things they were carrying.

'She's all we've got,' said Hetty.

The sea and sky were growing darker, the air colder. She ran through her preparations one final time. She'd stowed the blankets, and the old spare sail she'd brought to pull over the woman if there was rain, and they both had thick clothes and jackets and hats, and water to drink, and the bread and cheese she'd taken from the cottage.

She prayed there was enough food for the voyage, but there was precious little storage space in *Baby Dolphin*. She stepped onto the track that ran along the top of the beach, then picked her way down onto the shingle. The whispers began again and the woman stiffened, as though she had heard them.

'Nearly there,' said Hetty.

She reached *Baby Dolphin* and looked down at the woman again.

'I'm going to put you on the shingle,' she said. 'Just for a moment while I pull *Baby Dolphin* into the water.'

She placed the woman carefully down and tugged at the bow. *Baby Dolphin* was heavier than usual with the blankets and food and water, and the extra sail, all wedged under thwarts and up in the bow, plus the anchor, oars, rudder, and tiller. With something of a struggle, Hetty pulled the dinghy into the water. It felt cold but strangely bracing. She looked up at the cliff and spoke to the hermit of Mora.

'Give us your blessing,' she said. 'We need it.'

*Baby Dolphin* was floating comfortably now, small waves lapping against the hull. Hetty pulled the dinghy back so that her nose dug into the shingle, then she let go, ran to the woman on the shore, and bent down to pick her up—then stopped.

'I wish I knew your name,' she said.

The woman looked up.

'Rosa.'

'Rosa?' said Hetty. 'Is that your name?'

'Stars.'

Hetty stared at her, then she realized that the woman was gazing past her. She turned and looked up—and there they were: ghostly stars, just visible in the chamber of the night.

'Let's sail,' she said.

She carried the woman to the water's edge. *Baby Dolphin* had started to float clear of the beach but she was still close. Hetty waded through the shallows and stopped alongside. She'd already made a space for the woman near the bow, lengthwise along the bottom boards, her feet towards the stern and her back supported by the forward thwart. She helped the woman into the boat and settled her in position, then stood back, aware of a pounding in her chest.

She gripped the gunwale and stared over the black water. No whispers came from it now. She peered up at the sky and saw more stars breaking through. They seemed dim and cold. She thought of the hermit again and turned to the cliff. A figure was standing at the top. She stared, wondering. The outline was clear, even in the darkness. It was an old man but no one she had ever seen on Mora.

'Give us your blessing,' she said.

But the old man was gone.

She turned *Baby Dolphin* to face the sea and climbed in. The water was growing darker by the minute but more stars were breaking out above. She made the woman as comfortable as she could, then she shipped the rudder and hoisted the sail. The north-easterly breeze nudged them out of the bay and Mora slipped away.

# Chapter 22

She didn't glance round, not once. She knew that the moment she looked back, she would turn back. So she looked at the woman instead.

'You can be my eyes,' she said. 'You can say goodbye to Mora.'

The woman said nothing, nor did her eyes stray towards the island. They remained on Hetty, watching quietly, as *Baby Dolphin* cut through the night sea. The water stayed calm, the breeze steady. Hetty checked the little compass she had brought with her. Due south was the direction they needed to go and if the wind remained constant, they should see Brinda some time around noon tomorrow.

Haga, she knew, was well beyond their reach. She'd learned enough about the little mainland port from things Mackie had told her down the years to realize that: fifty-two miles as the crow flew, but much further once the other islands in the archipelago and their various rocks and reefs had been skirted or negotiated, and further still if wind and tide were troublesome, which they usually were, Mackie said.

So it had to be Brinda: the nearest island and a risky enough voyage in itself for a boat this small. If she missed Brinda, all was not lost. Another half-day should take them to the next two islands in the chain, Styr to the east, Faerde to the west, and beyond these two to the rest of the archipelago. She felt sure she couldn't miss all of them.

But Brinda was the landfall she wanted. She could just about picture the island from what Grandy and others had told her, and she knew Mackie had a trading friend there called Ivan, who owned a large, seagoing boat. If she could just reach Brinda and find this man, she might be able to persuade him to carry the woman to Haga in his boat. She could also tell him about Mackie's desperate need for timber.

'Rosa,' she said suddenly.

The woman looked at her without a word.

'You gave me the name Rosa,' said Hetty. 'Is that what you're called?'

The woman's eyes were bright against the darkness. Again there was no answer. Hetty trimmed the sail. The wind had started to increase, and it was veering too. She hoped this wouldn't continue. She needed as much north in the wind as possible, but it was turning fickle already. The woman shivered.

'Are you cold?' said Hetty.

She'd wrapped the woman inside two blankets, so that only her face was visible, but a second shiver soon followed the first. She put the helm down and let *Baby Dolphin* drift, then crawled forward.

'Are you all right?' she said.

'Rosa.'

'You said it again,' said Hetty. 'Is that your name?'

No answer.

'Let's get you warmer.'

She reached into the bow. There was another blanket there which she'd brought for herself, and the spare sail. She draped the blanket over the woman's body, then tucked it in underneath. *Baby Dolphin* rocked in the swell, her sail flapping.

'Let's have some bread and cheese,' said Hetty.

She pulled out the box and opened it. The woman saw the food and turned her head away.

'Don't you want it?' said Hetty.

She broke off a small piece of bread, put it to her mouth, nibbled a tiny bit, held out the rest. The woman ignored it and looked up at the sail, still flapping above them.

'You must eat,' said Hetty.

She took another nibble at the bread and again held out the rest. The woman looked back at her but did not take it. Hetty broke off a minute piece and steered it towards the woman's face. To her surprise, the mouth opened. She put the bread carefully in.

'Well done.'

The woman chewed the bread and swallowed it.

'Let's have some more,' said Hetty.

The woman looked up at the sail again.

'All right,' said Hetty. 'We'll eat again later.'

She pulled the blankets more tightly round the woman and steered *Baby Dolphin* back on her southerly course, but as each hour passed, her anxiety grew. The wind was not only growing stronger but it was continuing to veer. If it went much further round the compass, they would struggle to stay on course for Brinda and have to tack to avoid being pushed down to the west of the archipelago.

She gripped the tiller, thinking hard. She'd so hoped for a straight run south from Mora. Beating in a small boat against a rising wind was the last thing she wanted. *Baby Dolphin* heeled under a sudden gust. Hetty eased the sheet but a dusting of spray came over the bow. The wind veered further, growing in strength. She checked the compass again. They were still on course but it seemed only a matter of time before she'd be forced to claw east for a while before heading south again.

She looked at the woman: still wrapped in the blankets, and apparently sleeping; but then she opened her eyes. Hetty didn't speak. The luff of the sail was crinkling again and she could feel the tug in the tiller. As she'd feared, the wind was veering once more. She trimmed the sail and found they were heading south-west. She put the helm down and went about.

The woman seemed unconcerned by the change of direction, the flapping of the sail, the opposite side of the hull rising as *Baby Dolphin* heeled on the new tack. She remained as she had been all along, propped against the thwart, the blankets still wrapped about her. But the boat was shipping more spray. Hetty let out the sheet and scrambled forward.

'Here,' she said.

She pulled out the spare sail, wrapped it round the woman, and straightened up. The boat was now rocking violently. She clambered back to the helm and brought *Baby Dolphin* back on course, heading as close-hauled as possible. But this was now proving difficult. With the wind growing stronger by the minute, the boat was heeling ever-more sharply.

A volley of squalls struck. Hetty spilt the wind to steady the dinghy, but it made little difference. *Baby Dolphin* was struggling to stay upright. She spilt more wind. The hull eased downwards but only a little, and more spray burst over the bow. The woman gave a moan.

'Don't be frightened,' called Hetty.

She bore away, steering across the wind this time. It was obvious that they couldn't beat into a storm as strong as this. But the new course felt no better. Even with the sail well out, they were heeling violently and shipping more spray. There was nothing else for it but to run before the wind. She bore away further and the spray eased at last.

But they were now rolling dangerously. They were also heading north-east into empty ocean. Hetty crouched over the helm, aware of a new fear. The dinghy was moving much too fast. She watched the bow rear and plunge, rear and plunge. Mackie had told her stories of sailing boats sunk by mountainous following seas.

She threw a glance behind her. Already the rollers were building up, their frosty peaks glistening in the night. One by one they lifted the stern, coursed along the hull and swept past the bow, the boat rocking as they churned by. Somehow Hetty kept *Baby Dolphin* on course.

An hour later the woman was still wrapped in the blankets and spare sail, but her eyes were now wide, her face wet, and her hair streamed out like a river of snow. She'd been whimpering for some time. But Hetty did not dare leave the helm to attend to her. Even in the last few minutes, the storm had worsened.

Her arms now ached from the strain of tiller and sheet. The boat was moving so fast it was hard to steer. She peered round at the waves building up astern. They were huge now and she knew any one of them could sink *Baby Dolphin* if she lost control of the tiller. But now, to her horror, she saw the woman crawling towards her.

'Go back!' she shouted. 'Go back!'

The woman continued, the blankets and spare sail falling off her.

'Stop!'

The woman stopped, looked at her, then sat down on the bottom boards.

'I'll cover you up again in a moment,' Hetty shouted. 'When this big wave's gone by.'

But it was not to be. The wave rolled in, the stern rose, and there was a sickening crack. A moment later the mast snapped at the base and carried away over the bow. Hetty screamed.

'No!'

*Baby Dolphin* skewed round in the turmoil of the wave. Hetty yanked at the helm in an effort to bring the boat back on course, but there was no response. A hand clutched her shin.

'Not now!' she yelled.

She stared at the mess in the bows. The mast had broken clean away and fallen over the side, together with the yard and sail, but the halyard, sheet, and shrouds still kept everything attached to the hull. She glanced quickly round. *Baby Dolphin* was broadside on to the waves but there was a brief gap in the rollers. She scrambled forward, spray flying into her as the bow bucked and rolled in the swell.

Somehow she reached through the tangle of ropes and found the edge of the sail. She pulled; it wouldn't move. She gripped the wooden yard that ran along the top of the sail and tugged. It too resisted. She tugged again, and this time it yielded a few inches. From behind her came a scream. She shot a glance over her shoulder and saw the woman reaching towards her.

'Stay there!' she shouted. 'Don't move!'

She went on pulling. The yard was out of the water now, and with it part of the sail, the mast still beyond reach but attached to the cradle of ropes. She stared at the mess, tempted to cut the ropes and let everything go, but she knew she had to salvage what she could. There might just be a chance to use it.

If they survived this.

But time was running out. The boat was writhing in the wreckage of a new wave that had somehow surged past unnoticed. Luckily it hadn't been one of the monsters, but

Hetty knew that one of those would arrive soon. The woman screamed again from the stern. Hetty ignored her and went on pulling. At last she had the yard in the boat, and most of the sail, but she was tangled in ropes now and the mast was half-over the side and crashing against the hull.

The woman screamed a third time. Hetty looked round and saw a new wave thundering in. She saw the hull lift, felt the shock and shudder of the boat as the roller raced by underneath. As the hull fell again, the end of the mast swung over the bow and crashed into the side of her head. She gave a shriek of pain and fell into the chaos of ropes, sail, and yard, the mast rolling on top of her, half-in, half-out of the boat.

She struggled back upright, pulled her knife from its sheath, cut everything clear, and threw the mast overboard. The woman was now screaming without pause. Hetty took no notice, bundled the yard, sail and what was left of the ropes into the bottom of the boat, and clambered back to the stern.

The woman was curled up there now, silent but trembling. Beyond the boat more waves were building and *Baby Dolphin* was still broadside on to them. Hetty seized one of the oars, paddled the stern round to face them, then thrust the oar back into the boat as the next roller drove in. The stern lifted, higher, higher, then, just as the boat seemed about to tip over, the wave creamed along the hull and passed beyond the bow.

Hetty slumped at the helm, breathing hard, and searched for the next roller. Even in the darkness she could see the procession of them overhauling the boat, peaks glistening as before. She felt a hand touch her foot and looked down. The woman was still curled up on the bottom boards close by, but she had turned to face the stern and was now hugging Hetty's leg.

'I know,' said Hetty. 'You're frightened. I'm sorry I shouted at you.'

To her surprise, the woman smiled—a strange, sudden smile that seemed to come from nowhere and for no obvious reason. It quickly went again, but the woman continued to look up at her.

'I'll take care of you,' said Hetty.

But there was no time to say more. The next wave was already lifting the stern. She met it as well as she could, but it was hard now to control the boat without the momentum from the sail. They were no longer moving at terrifying speed, but with so little steerage way the boat felt even more vulnerable. The wave surged past, in spite of her fears, and so did the next, and the one after that; and so it continued for the rest of the night.

And somehow *Baby Dolphin* did not founder.

# Chapter 23

Dawn brought a grey sky and a riven sea, flecked with white caps, and no sight of land. They drove on before the wind, Hetty at the helm, the woman still clinging to her leg. Hetty checked over her shoulder. The procession of waves was still there, but there was no doubt that their size and severity had diminished. The wind, too, had decreased a little, though it was still strong. She bent down to the woman.

'I'm going to bale out the water,' she said. 'Then I'll get you warm again.'

The woman pressed her face into Hetty's thigh. Hetty eased it back.

'Stay here,' she said.

She took the baler, scooped out as much water as she could, then gathered the blankets and the old spare sail. The blankets were drier than she'd expected. The spare sail seemed to have kept the worst of the spray off them. She found the small towel she'd packed in the stern locker and wiped the woman's face and neck.

'Better?'

'Yes,' said the woman.

Hetty gave a start. She hadn't for one moment expected a reply. She pushed the towel back in the locker, took the driest of the blankets and wrapped it round the woman's body.

'How's that?'

There was no answer this time.

'Let's get you even warmer,' said Hetty.

She wrapped the other blankets round the woman, then the spare sail.

'That's better.'

'Better,' said the woman.

Hetty smiled.

'I love it when you say things,' she said. 'Let's have some food and water.'

She fetched the bread, cheese, and water, wondering what games she would have to play to entice the woman to eat and drink, but to her surprise none were needed. The woman ate the bread and cheese without a word, then drank the water too.

'Well done,' said Hetty.

She ate and drank her own portion, then looked about her. The movement of the boat was changing. It was lumpy now rather than frantic and she sensed a clash of wind and tide. She returned to her place at the helm and *Baby Dolphin* limped on towards the north-east.

Two hours later the wind had fallen to a breeze. It had also started to veer again, and as the day progressed, it continued its passage round the compass. By noon it was almost due west; three hours later Hetty detected the first traces of north in it. But by then it was almost dead, and the sea was calm too. She stared about her.

There was no sign of life out here, not even birds. The sea stretched away to a stony horizon. *Baby Dolphin* was barely moving at all. What forward motion she possessed was roughly towards the east. Hetty looked at the woman again. She was gazing towards the southern horizon, almost as though she knew Haga lay in that direction.

Hetty studied the face. There was an intelligence in it that the woman's mental confusion could not hide, and her moments of lucidity, fragmentary though they were, only added to that impression. The woman turned suddenly.

'I'm sorry,' said Hetty. 'Did you feel me watching you?'

A pained expression appeared on the woman's face.

'Are you all right?' said Hetty. 'What is it?'

Then she understood.

'I'll help you,' she said. 'Come on. Let's take off the blankets and sail and get you to the stern.'

With some difficulty she helped the woman relieve herself, then discreetly took care of her own needs.

'Now then,' she said, 'let's get you warm again.'

She started to wrap the first of the blankets round the woman's body. Then she stopped.

'What have you got in your hand?' she said.

But she'd already guessed. She stared at the closed fist. It was just as it had been back on Mora. Somehow in all that had happened, she'd forgotten about the sea glass. It was hard to believe that the woman had kept it, unnoticed.

'Can I see?' she said.

The woman uncurled her fingers and there was the sea glass in the palm of her hand.

'May I take it?' said Hetty. 'Just for a minute?'

She felt a desperate urge to touch the sea glass again. She hoped her voice did not betray how close she was to tears. But the woman held it out at once.

'Faces,' she said.

Hetty stared at her.

'Faces,' said the woman again.

Hetty took the sea glass and held it up. The two images were still there, the girl that looked like her, the man she did not know.

'Yes,' she murmured.

She felt a hand on her own and looked up.

'You want the sea glass back, don't you?' she said.

The woman was already feeling for it with her thin fingers.

'Here,' said Hetty. 'I just wanted to touch it again.'

The woman closed it once more inside her hand. Hetty wrapped the blankets and spare sail round her again, then peered over the sea. It was hardly moving now. She left the tiller and settled herself in the bottom of the boat, then put an arm round the woman's shoulder and pulled her close.

A stillness fell upon the sea. As dusk closed round them, the cold deepened, and Hetty watched the approach of night with dread. If the chill grew more intense, she knew the woman might not make it to the morning; and she too might not. She was shivering badly now. She felt a nudge against her side and looked round.

'No,' said the woman.

'What's wrong?' said Hetty.

The woman was trying to pull off the blankets and sail.

'But you need those things on,' said Hetty. 'To keep you warm.'

The woman went on fighting the blankets and sail.

'All right,' said Hetty. 'I'll help you.'

She removed the sail, then peeled off the blankets one by one.

'This isn't a good idea,' she said.

She stared down at the bundle in her arms, wondering what to do next, but now the woman was reaching for the blankets again. Hetty looked up at her angrily.

'Now what?' she said, but then it became clear. 'You're trying to cover us both up.'

The woman went on tugging at the blanket.

'It won't be big enough for both of us,' said Hetty. 'None of the blankets are. That's why I wanted you to have them.'

'No!'

The woman stared at her suddenly, a fiery will in her eyes.

'All right,' said Hetty. 'We'll share everything, but let me do it. I'm better at this than you.'

She pulled the blankets tightly round them both, making sure the woman had most. Her own left side was partly exposed, but it was better than she'd expected and she already felt the blessing of new warmth. The spare sail covered them both easily, and that helped too. The woman leaned towards her without coaxing and they huddled together on the bottom boards.

Night fell and the cold increased. Hetty pulled the woman closer, and as she did so, she felt something hard dig into her side. She knew what it was. She felt for the woman's fist and closed her hand round it.

'I know what you're holding,' she said quietly.

The woman's eyes met hers.

'Keep it safe,' said Hetty.

She stared towards the stern of the boat. The tiller was flicking from side to side as the swell played upon the rudder. Night enfolded them, the cold deepening further. To her surprise, the woman fell asleep: an easy, childlike sleep, as if without care. Around midnight, rain started, and the woman opened her eyes.

'It's all right,' said Hetty. 'Only rain.'

She unwrapped the spare sail, then pulled it over the top of them and down at the sides.

'Like a little tent, isn't it?' she said.

The rain pattered on the top of the sail. Hetty peered round. In the closed space all was black, but she could see the outline of the woman's head, and after a few moments, the glint of her eyes. The rain grew heavier, drumming sleet-like upon the sail and running down the sides to the bottom boards. The woman moved nearer. Hetty put an arm round her and again felt the small fist push into her side.

'Let's have something to eat,' she said.

She reached behind her with her free hand and pulled out the box with the bread and cheese. The woman looked at it indifferently, but she ate everything Hetty gave her, and drank some of the water from the flask. Hetty took a little for herself, then replaced the things under the thwart.

There was not much left now.

She lay back, listening to the rain beating on the sail, and the woman's breathing, close to her ear; and somehow she fell asleep. When she woke again, all was silent and black, and for a few moments she thought she was on Mora, waking in her room; then a lurch of the hull jolted her mind back to where she was. She glanced to the side. The woman was asleep, her head drooping. Hetty lifted the side of the sail and peeped out.

Night was still heavy upon them, and so was the chill, but the rain had stopped and the wind was picking up again. She crawled out from under the sail and sat in the stern, gauging the breeze. It wasn't fierce but it was steady, and already *Baby Dolphin* was moving with it. She checked the compass, tested the wind again: it was coming from the north. She turned and stared the other way, wary of hope.

'Try it,' she said to herself. 'Mackie would.'

She checked under the old spare sail. The woman had curled up on the bottom boards and was still sleeping. Hetty covered her again, then took *Baby Dolphin*'s sail, still attached to its wooden yard, and crawled with it into the bow. Before her was the broken mast stump, still in its slot. She frowned. It was hard to see how this could work.

She thought of Mackie again, pulled out the broken stump and threw it over the side, then pushed the end of the wooden yard into the empty slot. It made a poor replacement mast. Not only was it loose in the slot but it was shorter than the original mast so a great deal of the lower part of the sail fell uselessly into the boat. On an impulse she gathered this crumpled segment together and forced as much of it as she could into the slot around the sides of the yard.

It was a messy solution but it did give the yard some stability. To strengthen it further she ran the now redundant halyard from the yard down into the bow and made it fast to act as a stay; then she looked over the sail. It was an outlandish rig: a small, triangular piece of cloth, just over half the size of what it used to be. But it would have to do. She led the sheet back to the stern and sat down.

'Please work,' she said.

She took the helm and trimmed the sail. At first nothing seemed to happen; then, with some hesitation, *Baby Dolphin* turned towards the south.

# *Chapter 24*

They sailed through the night, a laboured passage with the boat rolling from the clumsy pull of the jury sail. The woman went on sleeping, in spite of the sounds and motion of the boat, and Hetty was glad to be able to focus on the sea. It was growing lively again and she'd already had to deal with several rogue waves that had raced up unseen in the dark. But at dawn the woman pushed aside the old spare sail and peered out.

'We're sailing,' said Hetty.

The woman twisted round to stare over the bow.

'We're heading south,' said Hetty, 'but that's all I can tell you. I've got no idea where we are. We might see one of the eastern islands of the archipelago, Styr or Broma maybe. I don't think we're anywhere near Brinda. We've been blown too far east. And Mora's way behind us. To the north or north-west, I think. And we can't go and find it because we can't go against the wind with this jury rig. So we've got to head south.'

She had no idea why she was chattering on like this. The woman was still staring over the bow and gave no indication of having understood or even heard her.

'South,' said the woman suddenly.

'Yes,' said Hetty.

To her surprise she saw the woman turn back and start crawling towards her.

'What's wrong?' she said.

The woman simply reached under the thwart, took the baler and started scooping out some of the water that had come in during the night. Hetty watched, unsure what to think. The woman took no notice of her and continued baling with quiet, methodical movements. When she'd finished, she put down the baler and burrowed under the thwart again.

'What are you looking for?' said Hetty.

The woman turned round, holding the food box.

'Are you hungry?' said Hetty.

She hadn't planned to touch this just yet. There was so little food left that they needed to make it last. But the woman was crawling back to her again, cradling the box. As she drew closer, Hetty saw that the left hand was still closed in a fist. The woman stopped in front of her and pulled the top off the box. Hetty glanced inside at the few pieces of bread; the single chunk of cheese.

'You start,' she said. 'But save a bit for later.'

The woman tore off a piece of bread and held it up. Hetty shook her head.

'It's yours.'

'No!'

The woman sat up straight; and there was the fire in her eyes again.

'It's yours,' said Hetty.

She tried to think of a ploy.

'I can't eat now. I've got to steer the boat.'

The woman pushed the bread towards her.

'I've got to steer the boat,' said Hetty. 'I can eat later.'

But the bread was pressing against her mouth now. Reluctantly she accepted it and started chewing. The woman watched her closely, and when the bread had gone down, she tore off a second piece and pushed that forward too.

'Your turn,' said Hetty.

'Eat.'

'I'm not hungry.'

'Eat.'

*Baby Dolphin* gave a lurch as a larger wave shouldered the bow to starboard. Hetty corrected the course, glad of an excuse to ignore the food. But the woman was still pushing it towards her. Hetty glanced towards the bow, searching for another wave, but there were no further diversions. She opened her mouth and accepted the bread.

'I'm eating, see?' she said.

She was startled by the tone of her voice. It was the same tone she used to Grandy when she was pretending to eat, promising to eat, refusing to eat. She studied the woman's face. It had subtly changed. The frailty was as marked as ever, yet another quality had appeared: something implacable, that made her think of Grandy again.

'Your turn now,' she said.

The woman simply pushed more bread at her.

'You must eat,' said Hetty. 'You —'

But she could say no more. The bread was in her mouth, stopping further words, and the woman was watching closely as if to make sure she ate it. She chewed the bread slowly, swallowed it and frowned.

'I'm supposed to be protecting you,' she said. 'Not the other way round.'

But the woman did not appear to be listening. She was poking round the food box again. She pulled out the last of the cheese.

'I don't want any more,' said Hetty.

'Eat!'

The woman's eyes were dark and strong.

'You're frightening,' said Hetty, 'when you look at me like that.'

'Eat.'

The word was softer now, the eyes too. But there was no mistaking their intention.

'We've both got to eat,' said Hetty. 'Not just me.'

The woman steered the cheese towards Hetty's mouth.

'I'll eat half of it,' said Hetty.

She bit off half and started to chew it. The woman simply waited for her to swallow, then pushed the other half forward. Hetty shook her head.

'I can't,' she said. 'It's not right.'

The cheese was close to her mouth now.

'I can't eat everything we've got left,' she said.

She felt the woman's hand on her wrist, felt the cheese push against her lips, and she knew there was nothing else for it.

'All right,' she said quietly.

She opened her mouth and ate the cheese. The woman watched her as before, then fumbled round for the last scraps of bread, and held these out too. Hetty ate them without a word. The woman found the water flask, unstopped it, held it up. Hetty drank, then twisted her face away.

'Your turn now,' she said.

But the woman simply stopped the flask, slid everything back under the thwart, and turned to stare forward. Hetty watched her with a strange disquiet, guilty over the food she'd just eaten, yet also aware—perhaps for the first time—of the will that had kept this woman alive, and perhaps was now keeping her alive too.

They sailed on, the bow tracing wild shapes, sometimes against the sea, sometimes the sky. In the far distance the horizon stretched to a vacuous infinity. Hetty looked over the boat. *Baby Dolphin* was enveloped in a turbulence of sound, wrought by waves and the stiffening breeze. The sail tugged and flapped, jerking the sheet and straining the wooden yard, which somehow had remained in its slot, and the hull drove on through the deepening wave-troughs.

There were more white-caps now and spray bursting over the bow. Hetty gripped the tiller and sheet, aware of *Baby Dolphin*'s increasing vulnerability, yet the boat drove on faster than ever, revelling, it seemed, in the growing savagery of wind and sea. A crash in the bows and the dinghy plunged down the side of a foaming wave; another crash and she rose again as a new wave lifted her to its bubbling peak.

She was handling the seas well, in spite of their size, and the jury mast and sail were holding firm, but Hetty knew this wouldn't last if things grew rougher. Some of the stronger gusts had already tested the rig to its limits. She was worried about the spray too. They were shipping more and more now, thanks to the sharper configuration of the waves and the mad motion of the hull. The woman turned towards her and shivered.

'You need the blankets round you again,' said Hetty. 'And the spare sail.'

The woman crawled away towards the thwart, then returned, holding one of the blankets. A plunge of the bow and more spray came flying over the side. Hetty forced her mind back to the boat, the sail, the next breaking wave. But here was the woman, reaching out with the blanket.

'Not now,' said Hetty. 'I've got to watch the boat.'

*Baby Dolphin* was surfing down the slope of a wave, the sail bulging with the strain, the yard bent at the top. Hetty watched nervously. These seas were shorter than the ones last night but they were also more aggressive, and much of the time they clashed with each other in skirmishes of leaping water. She needed her full concentration to deal with this. But now she could feel the woman spreading the blanket over her legs.

'Not over me,' she said quickly. 'Wrap it round yourself.'

The woman ignored her and carried on. Hetty put her mind back on the boat. But even as she guided *Baby Dolphin* through the broken seas, she felt the woman spread blanket after blanket over her legs, and the old spare sail, and then crawl under herself. She waited for a clearer patch of water, then looked down. Only the woman's head was visible, facing the oncoming spray, though Hetty could feel the small body quivering against her legs. She leaned down and kissed the top of the woman's head.

'Thank you,' she said.

*Baby Dolphin* crashed on, through the morning and afternoon and on to a new dusk and a new night, the motion unrelenting. Hetty yearned for it to stop now, or at least ease, but there seemed no sign of it. They were still heading south, as they had been doing throughout the day, and she knew that if land was to be found, it was most likely to be in that direction. But darkness had shut off the horizon, and wind and sea were as hostile as ever.

Yet an hour later she sensed the change. Less strain in the sheet, less spray over the bow. *Baby Dolphin* drove on, but the commotion of the previous hours was waning. She peered up at the sky. No moon or stars, just islands of cloud. The sea, too, had grown sombre, with barely a white cap showing. All that broke the endless dark was an occasional flash of foam down the side of the hull.

She scanned the sea again. It was definitely less fierce than it had been, though she knew she had to be careful with the night so dense. The sail flapped suddenly, then filled again. Hetty glanced at it. The wind was continuing to fall, though it was still constant enough to push them on, and still from the north.

*Baby Dolphin* sailed on, more gently now that the wind was losing strength, and after a while the woman fell asleep. Hetty longed to do the same, but she knew she dare not. They had to sail while there was still wind. They had to try to find land. But some time in the early morning, the breeze died altogether.

And the whispers began.

# *Chapter 25*

When she first became aware of them, she had the curious feeling that they'd been audible for some time and that some other part of her had been listening to them without her consciously knowing. She let go of the tiller and sheet, useless in this unexpected calm, and sat there, as still as the sail, and the boat, and the sea, and the sleeping woman huddled against her.

Around her was a dark space. It was like a vast room with an airy dome and a watery floor, but no walls to see or sense in any direction. She could have been floating in nothingness, and for a while she wondered if she was. The whispers went on, wordlessly.

'Who's speaking?' she said.

The surface of the water glistened for a moment. The woman murmured but did not wake. Hetty tidied the blankets and sail over them both and felt the small fist push into her side. She looked down at the woman's face but the eyes remained closed. The fist nudged her again. She felt for it under the blanket.

There it was, strangely insistent. She felt the fingers open, the palm press against hers, and now the woman's other hand had come round, guiding; and Hetty understood. She took the sea glass and closed her fingers round it, and the woman let go and returned to her sleep.

The whispers went on, the woman's breaths merging with the sound. Hetty brought the sea glass from under

179

the covers and peered at it in the darkness. The images were impossible to make out. She went on staring, hoping her eyes would adjust. She felt a yearning to see the faces again, but night shielded the secrets of the glass.

She wondered why the woman had chosen this moment to give the sea glass back, having guarded it so ferociously. The whispers grew fainter. The woman stirred, just a shift of her posture, then slept on. Hetty watched her for a few minutes, then stared over the sea again.

It was like a different ocean from the one they had traversed from Mora. The surface was so smooth and still it was hard to believe that the water had ever moved. She thought of the terrifying waves *Baby Dolphin* had struggled through to get to where they were now, and wondered how many times she and the woman had nearly died.

'Maybe you'll still take us,' she said to the sea.

The whispers grew louder again. She listened hard, certain that there must be words, if only she could catch them; but as always, they eluded her. She stroked the sea glass, held it up, and to her surprise found she could see the images again, in spite of the darkness—but everything had changed. Where before she had seen a girl like her and an old man, and before that the woman herself, now she saw a crowd of faces pushing into every scrap of space.

'Are you all drowned?' she said to them.

None of the faces were clear. She ran her eye over them, trying to make out the details, but only the outlines were visible. *Baby Dolphin* rocked for a few moments, then was still. The whispers died away and silence fell. All that broke it was the woman's breathing. Hetty rested her head against the woman's.

'I'm glad you're sleeping,' she murmured.

She looked down to make sure the woman had not woken, then lowered her voice further.

'I wish I could.'

She gave a sigh.

'But I'm frightened I might never wake up again.'

She pulled the blanket and spare sail more tightly around them.

'This is the farthest from home I've ever been,' she went on. 'I've never been out of sight of Mora. I've never wanted to. Not after the sea took my mother and father.'

She thought of the sea glass again, but didn't look at it.

'They drowned when I was a tiny girl,' she said. 'I don't remember any of it. I was too small. They went out in one of the boats to try to rescue some people who got into difficulty off Mora. We lost four from the island that day, Grandy said. My mother and father and two others. One of them was Dolly's husband. The other was Per's son. And the people in the other boat drowned too. No bodies got washed up. The sea kept them all.'

She squeezed the sea glass tight.

'That's Mora's history,' she said. 'A history of loss. Grandy and the others say you have to be strong. It's the island way. Bury the dead quickly and get on with living. But I can't be like that. I keep hoping . . .'

She took a slow breath.

'I keep hoping for something I can't have.'

'Voices,' said the woman suddenly.

Hetty lifted her head. The woman opened her eyes and looked round at her.

'Voices,' she said again.

Hetty listened, but all she heard was a deep, pervasive silence.

'I can't hear any voices,' she said.

The woman turned and stared towards the bow.

'Is that where they're coming from?' said Hetty.

The woman didn't answer. Hetty listened again. As before, all was silent, but something else was happening: she could feel a cool touch on the back of her neck. A moment later the sail fluttered. It was more of a breath than a breeze, but it was something, and still from the north. She thrust the sea glass into her pocket, climbed back to the helm and trimmed the sail.

*Baby Dolphin* started to move, tentatively at first, then more steadily, heading south as before. Ten minutes later they were motionless again, but soon they were moving on, and so it continued for an hour or more, sailing and stopping, sailing and stopping, until finally the sailing ceased altogether, and they drifted once again.

This time Hetty did not resist sleep. The woman was curled up on the bottom boards, near to the thwart, her eyes closed. She'd simply lain there of her own accord, and whether she'd felt Hetty slip a blanket under her head, and spread another over her body, and the spare sail on top of that, there was no way of telling. She'd gone straight to sleep.

Hetty too curled up on the bottom boards, near to the helm. Above her the tiller stretched across her line of vision. It was still. She supposed that if the wind returned, some part of the boat would wake her, but wind seemed as far away as their chance of survival. She closed her eyes and dived into the darkness; only to sit up again with a start.

She stared about her. All was silent as before, yet she knew that couldn't be right. She'd heard what she'd heard: voices, calling her name. She looked about her, breathing furiously. Nothing moved on the surface of the water, nothing she could see anyway. She glanced at the woman. She'd said 'voices' earlier. She'd heard them too.

And so had Mackie's father. Hetty thought back to the story Mackie had told her of how his father had heard voices calling his name when he was alone on deck and *The Pride of Mora* was out of sight of land. They'd gone far out, looking for fish, and were heading home, having found none. The voices had come from the water, he said. They came back now, reaching through the darkness.

'Hetty,' they said.

She listened to them. They weren't loud or soft or male or female. They were just voices, calling from the sea. She called back to them.

'Who are you?'

The sail tugged at the sheet. The woman twisted on the bottom boards, her eyes still closed. Hetty stared about her, searching the sea. A breeze wafted over her, still from the north. The sail shivered and *Baby Dolphin* started to rock. Hetty slipped back to the helm and trimmed the sail. The boat moved on like a ghost.

'Hetty,' said the voices.

She hunched over the tiller, aching for rest but pent up with nameless fears. The motion of the boat was now so dreamlike it felt as though *Baby Dolphin* no longer needed her. The night sky was as dark as the sea and there was no hint of dawn. An hour of sailing passed, then the breeze died again, leaving them drifting in blackness. Hetty slumped to the bottom boards and plunged into sleep next to the woman. The last thing she remembered was the sound of her name, whispered by a thousand voices. When she woke again, it was dawn and they were floating at the base of a vast cliff.

And the woman was rigid.

# Chapter 26

'No,' said Hetty, 'you mustn't die.'

She felt for a pulse. It was there, but only just, and the woman was frighteningly still. She squeezed the arms, rubbed them gently.

'Wake, wake.'

The woman remained still, her eyes closed. Hetty rubbed the arms again.

'You kept me alive,' she said. 'You fed me and you kept me warm. And I'm going to keep you alive.'

The woman's eyes opened a fraction.

'There,' said Hetty. 'You're coming back to me.'

The face was still, but Hetty was sure she'd caught a smile in the eyes.

'You're not going to die,' she said. 'I won't let you.'

She looked up at the cliff. It was looming over them and there were huge rocks at the base, but she still had some sea room. She glanced quickly around her. There was no wind and the boat was bobbing in the swell. She scrambled up to the thwart, positioned her legs either side of the woman's body, and shipped the oars.

'You're going to live,' she said to the woman.

And she started to row. But the pull was hard. She could feel the current forcing her back towards the cliff. She rowed on with all her strength, and gradually brought *Baby Dolphin* clear. She rested on the oars, breathing heavily in the cold dawn, and studied the land.

It stretched away in both directions, but there was not enough light yet to see how far it went. This could be the mainland, but it could equally be one of the islands. She knew from what Mackie had told her that Brinda and Styr had high cliffs. She stared both ways, searching for a safe place to land.

But all was rock and cliff, as far as she could tell. The sail flapped, then fell limp again. She looked down. The woman had not stirred. She lay there, rigid as before, staring up into Hetty's face. Hetty smiled down at her.

'We've found land,' she said. 'I don't know where it is, but I'm going to get you to safety.'

Again, she caught the hint of a smile in the small, pale eyes.

She studied the land again. The grey of the dawn still made things hard to see. As far as she could tell, there was nowhere close by where they could get ashore; and there was another problem. Even if daylight revealed a landing place, she would never get the woman up the cliff. She wouldn't even get up it herself.

She tried to decide what to do. Neither direction offered any hope. She could row for miles and find nothing but high rock. From below her came a moan. She stared down and saw the woman breathing jerkily.

'It's all right,' she said quickly.

She reached down and stroked the woman's forehead. 'I'll take care of you.'

She straightened up and scanned the coast again. She had to make a choice. They couldn't just sit here, waiting for death. Then suddenly she saw it, far off to the right, just visible in the burgeoning light: a headland, and a short distance from it, a tall, rocky stack, and two smaller ones.

'The Three Spears,' she murmured.

As Mackie always called them. Grandy had mentioned them too, and so had others: the three rocky stacks that signalled the approach to Haga. In a fever of excitement she started to row towards them; but doubts were soon crowding in. There were rocky stacks in lots of places. Mora had two of her own off North Point, and she knew that Broma had several. Mackie had told her about them; and there were others too, he said, on the smaller, uninhabitable islands. He'd once drawn her a picture of one of them.

She rowed on, fighting the spectre of a barren shore on the other side of the headland. The spectre grew with every pull of the oars. To force it further back, she tried to remember the things Mackie had told her about Haga. A tiny port, he said, but a busy one. A little town above the sea, the main road twisting up between cliffs and away to the rest of the world.

The rest of the world.

Mackie always called it that.

But he was wrong, she decided. It wasn't the rest of the world. It was another world: a world she had never known or wanted any part of. She rowed on, the oars rasping, her breaths harsh and laboured. She glanced over her shoulder. The distance to the headland seemed almost greater than when she had first started rowing towards it. She drove herself on, determined not to look again for at least a quarter of an hour.

It was much later than that when she did.

And the headland was just a short distance away.

She rested on her oars again, almost spent. The woman had not moved or spoken, but her eyes were still open, and she was peering up into Hetty's face, as she had done all along. Hetty looked down at her and forced another smile.

'Wind,' said the woman.

Hetty stared about her. *Baby Dolphin* was being turned in an eddy of small waves, but there was no sense of a breeze. Then she caught it on her cheek: the faintest breath.

'Please,' she whispered.

The sail filled, fell idle, filled again. Hetty waited for the breeze to die, but it continued, still from the north. She unshipped the oars, slipped back to the tiller and trimmed the sail. *Baby Dolphin* inched towards the outermost stack off the headland.

'We're sailing again,' she said to the woman. 'Sailing to Haga.'

'Haga,' said the woman.

But the spectre was back again, the image of a barren shore.

'Just get us round,' Hetty said to the wind.

It remained constant and gradually they drew nearer to the headland. Now that they were close to the stacks, she could see that they were immense columns of rock, even the smallest one at the end. She stood well out to give it plenty of room, wary of the white water that washed around the base, even in this calm sea.

Still the spectre taunted her, as she peered beyond the headland. All she saw was more cliffs rolling away towards the south: an unending wall against the sea, and against her. But they were not yet past the outermost stack. She sailed on, searching the shore that was continuing to open up—and there it was, tucked against the other side of the headland.

A small harbour.

'We've found it!' she said. 'We've found it!'

She looked at the woman. But the eyes were closed again.

'No!' said Hetty.

She scrambled forward and felt for the pulse. It was still just there. She stroked the woman's arms, whispered into her ear.

'We've found Haga. We've found your home.'

The woman made no response.

Hetty took the helm again.

'I'm getting you back to your people,' she said.

She rounded the stack and steered towards the harbour mouth. *Baby Dolphin* was moving more slowly now that the headland had cut off the wind, but there was still enough breeze to carry them on. The light was growing steadily and by it she could make out the small town nestling there, just as Mackie had described.

She could see houses, shops, a church, warehouses, boats in the harbour, a road running along the top of the quay and then climbing up through the town and away to the high ground beyond the cliff. Even at this early hour she could see people walking about and smoke rising from chimneys.

And now a boat putting off from the quay.

She stared at it—a long rowing boat, pulled by four powerful men and rapidly approaching. For a moment she felt wary of it. There was something in its sudden appearance and urgency that frightened her. The boat drew close and the men rested on their oars. All were bearded and about Mackie's age, and they were peering across the water with no sign of friendliness. One of them called over in a gruff voice.

'Where have you come from?'

'The island of Mora.'

'In that thing?'

'I need help,' she called. 'I have a woman with me who's very ill. And she's from Haga.'

No answer came back but she saw the men bend to their oars again. The boat drew swiftly closer.

'Don't come too near!' she shouted.

They took no notice and rowed right alongside, unshipping their oars at the last moment. Two of the men caught hold of *Baby Dolphin*'s gunwale. Hetty let go of the helm and stood over the woman's body.

'Don't hurt her!' she said.

The men were peering over.

'My God,' said one.

The biggest of the men looked at Hetty. She sensed he was the leader.

'Is she alive?' he said.

Hetty knelt down and felt for a pulse, willing the eyes to open again. They did not; but she felt a pulse.

'She's just alive.'

'Best we take her,' said the man. 'We can row quicker than you.'

'No,' said Hetty.

'You can sail in after us.'

'No!' Hetty glared at him, fists clenched. 'You're not separating us. She's sailing with me.'

The man frowned.

'Let her do it, Sten,' said one of the others. 'No time to waste.'

The man called Sten threw a glance at Hetty.

'Bring your boat alongside the quay. By those steps, see?'

Hetty nodded. The men pushed off without a word and waited for *Baby Dolphin* to pick up speed. Hetty fixed her attention on the harbour mouth, where a small crowd was gathering. She could see arms pointing towards her, and the glint of telescopes, and a small boy running back along the wall and up towards the town. Even from here she caught the sound of his high voice, calling.

'Grandfather!'

By the time she had entered the harbour, the walls on either side were packed with people staring down. She took little notice of them. Her attention was on the woman lying before her, face and body still, and now on a figure hobbling towards the quay from the top of the town. She recognized him at once as the old man she'd seen in the sea glass.

The little boy was walking beside him, holding his hand.

The men in the boat had rowed ahead and were moored by the steps up to the quay, but she saw that they had made a space for *Baby Dolphin*. She steered nervously towards them, aware of the eyes watching, and most of all those of the old man, now close to the quay itself.

At the last moment the wind failed. She clambered forward, stepping carefully round the woman, and lowered the sail; then she shipped the oars and rowed the last few yards to the quay. It too was now packed with people looking down, and the old man was waiting at the top of the steps. Hands gripped the side of the boat, and before she could protest, Sten had climbed over into *Baby Dolphin*.

'I'll take her from here.'

'Be careful,' she said.

'I will.'

He picked the woman up with great care, then turned and passed her to another of the men, who was standing at the base of the steps. Hetty watched, conscious of a desperate pain she had no words for. Sten had climbed out of the boat and taken the woman again, and he was now carrying her up the steps to the quay, watched by all.

The old man was waiting there, the boy at his side. Sten held her out, and the old man cradled her head for a few moments, then he straightened up and beckoned to Hetty. She climbed out of *Baby Dolphin* and onto the bottom step.

'Careful,' said one of the men from the rowing boat.

He was holding *Baby Dolphin* with one hand but he reached out with the other to catch Hetty by the arm and steady her.

'The boat,' she said to him. '*Baby Dolphin*.'

'She'll be fine.'

'Have you tied her up properly?'

'Of course I have.'

'But—'

'I'll look after her,' called a voice.

She peered up the steps and saw the boy staring down at her. He looked no more than seven or eight, but his face was sharp and earnest.

'I'll look after the boat,' he said.

She saw the old man nod.

'My grandson will take care of your boat.'

She made her way up the steps. The crowd was pressing round to watch but keeping a respectful distance. The woman was already being carried away on a stretcher with a blanket over her. Hetty stopped at the top of the steps. The boy walked up to her and took her left hand in both of his.

'I'm Per,' he said.

She took a long, tired breath.

'I knew someone called Per,' she said mechanically.

She stared past the boy at the ancient man.

'He was very old,' she added.

The boy let go of her hand and ran down the steps. She walked up to the man. He too took her hand.

'My name is Tor,' he said.

'I'm Hetty.'

She looked into his face: a calm, sad face.

'I've brought Rosa home,' she said.

He looked at her gravely, then squeezed her hand.

'Perhaps you have,' he answered.

# Chapter 27

For Hetty the next few hours were a blur. She remembered a blanket being draped round her, hands guiding her to the stretcher, the passage through the town, the silent faces, the unspeaking presence of Tor beside her; the quiet house, overlooking the sea, the friendly woman called Kristina taking her to a small room and helping her to undress and wash herself, and put on fresh-smelling night clothes, and eat and drink a little, and slip into bed.

But she could not sleep, tired though she was. She lay there, aware of the silence of the house and the murmur of the sea, and a deep disquiet within herself; and so she climbed out of bed and put on the dressing gown that had been left for her, and opened the door and walked down the corridor, following the sound of low voices, to the room at the end.

She knew what she would find within. She opened the door and stepped through. The woman lay in the bed, her eyes closed. Tor sat beside her in a chair with Kristina and another man standing behind him. Curtains were drawn across and candles burning at the foot of the bed. Kristina walked quickly over.

'You're meant to be sleeping, Hetty.'

'I've got to be here. Please let me stay.'

'Of course,' said Kristina. 'We all understand.'

She took Hetty by the hand and led her to the bed. Tor looked up.

'You haven't met my son, Hetty,' he said.

The other man smiled.

'My name is Aidan. I'm Kristina's husband. I understand you've met our little boy.'

'Per?'

'Yes.'

'He's looking after my boat.'

'I know,' said Aidan. 'He's a good lad. But my men are taking care of *Baby Dolphin* now. I've told them to lift her out of the water and give her a new mast and sail. And clean her thoroughly, of course.'

'Thank you.'

'It's the least we can do.'

They all turned to the bed.

'Is she still alive?' said Hetty.

'For a little while longer,' said Tor.

'Is there anything we can do?'

'We can sit with her.'

Hetty looked round at the old man.

'Is it all right if I sit on the edge of the bed?'

'Of course,' said Tor.

'I don't mean to be disrespectful. I could get a chair.'

'Sit there,' said Tor. 'She'd want that.'

'Thank you.'

Hetty sat on the edge of the bed. In the corner of her eye she sensed one of the candles flickering. She turned to look and saw for the first time a wood fire burning in the grate on the far side of the room. She looked back at the still face of the woman. It seemed somehow different; she wasn't sure why. They had cleaned her and washed her, and tidied her hair and made her look as beautiful as they could, but it wasn't that. It was something else.

'She looks peaceful,' she said eventually.

'She is peaceful,' said Tor. 'Thanks to you, Hetty.'

She looked round at him.

'I didn't give her peace. I just brought her home.'

'You did more than that,' said Tor.

Kristina and Aidan pulled up chairs and sat down.

'Can you tell us what happened?' said Aidan.

She thought for a moment, sifting what to say and what to conceal, then told them of the great storm, the destruction of *The Pride*, the small boat crashing on the island, the woman's fight for life, the friendship they had formed, the secret decision she had taken, the voyage back to Haga—but nothing of superstition or hostility or a dream of ancient evil; and they listened without interrupting. When she'd finished, she realized she was holding one of the woman's hands. She gave a start and let go.

'You reached under the sheet and took it,' said Aidan, 'while you were talking to us.'

'I'm sorry.'

'Don't be,' said Aidan. 'Why don't you take it again?'

'Is it all right?'

'Of course it is.'

She took the woman's hand again. Aidan turned to Tor.

'Father, you should tell her.'

'I know.'

'Tell me what?' said Hetty.

'Our side of the story,' said Tor.

'She's your wife, isn't she?'

'Yes,' he said. 'We've been married for sixty-five years. I've no idea why she agreed to share her life with me. It's been a mystery to me from the beginning. What would a classical scholar see in an uneducated boat builder?'

'Father—' said Aidan.

'Let me go on,' said the old man.

He stared towards the bed.

'She gave up a lot to live with me, even came to settle in this little backwater where I was born and had my business. And while I built boats, she did her translations, and we were happy. Especially when we had a beautiful little girl.'

Hetty watched him, aware of a tension in his voice.

'But then we lost her,' he said quietly, 'when she was . . . ' He paused. 'How old are you, Hetty?'

'Fifteen.'

'She was fifteen. She looked like you too. Darker hair, but very like you.'

Hetty thought of the picture in the sea glass.

'How did she die?' she said, though she'd guessed the answer.

'She drowned,' said Tor. 'I had a new boat and we were sailing about a mile offshore. A freak wave caught her. It was nobody's fault, but my wife blamed herself. She was the nearest person on board. I told her there was nothing she could have done, but it made no difference. She's spent the rest of her life thinking it was her fault.'

The old man paused again.

'But we got on with living as best we could and then, a few years later, a wonderful thing happened.' He glanced at Aidan. 'We had a son. We never thought we'd be lucky again. We'd been trying for years without success and we were both getting older. But Aidan turned up, and he's given us great joy, and now he's taken over the boatbuilding business, and we have a lovely daughter-in-law and a grandson too, and I really thought my wife would finally be all right. But . . . '

He frowned.

'She started to lose her way, Hetty. You understand what I mean? I think you do. She went into a twilight and it just got darker and darker for her. In the last five years, she's almost been out of reach. And all she's been able to think about, it seems, is our daughter. I sometimes think that's all she remembers now.'

'She remembers you, Father,' said Aidan. 'And me. And Kristina. And Per.'

'Perhaps,' said Tor.

He stood up, hobbled to the fire and pushed on another log, then returned to his chair.

'We don't really know what happened,' he said to Hetty, 'but we can probably guess, now we've heard your story. As I just told you, my wife had been losing her way for some time. All she could talk about was the accident and the freak wave, and how she felt sure our daughter might still be alive somewhere out beyond the horizon, and we could find her if we just looked hard enough.'

He took a slow breath.

'She slipped out of the house one night while I was sleeping. I blame myself for that. I really do. I should have watched her more carefully.'

'It wasn't your fault, Father,' said Aidan.

'It was,' said Tor. 'I knew she was unstable. I should have stayed awake.'

'You're ninety years old, Pappa,' said Kristina. 'You're allowed to sleep.'

Tor shook his head and turned to Hetty again.

'She must have made her way down to the harbour. She had a small boat which we found missing in the morning.'

'*Semper Fidelis*,' said Hetty.

'Yes,' said Tor. 'I built the boat for her, back in the days when her mind was clear and she was safe on the water. She was good in a boat. She respected the sea, and she loved that little thing. She gave it its name, a Latin name. I forget what it means. She did tell me. Anyway,

I'm guessing she took the boat out that night to look for our daughter, and the storm drove her away from the land and she couldn't get back. Maybe she didn't want to. Most of the people of Haga put off in the morning to look for her. There was hardly a boat left in the harbour. But it was no good. The gale was too strong by then and we had to give up.'

'But somehow,' said Kristina, 'her boat found its way to Mora. Is that not a miracle? And Hetty finding her way back—that's a miracle too.'

'It's also an act of great courage,' said Aidan.

'Yes, it is,' said Tor. 'You're a very brave young woman, Hetty. I'll never be able to thank you enough. And we must get you back to your people as soon as possible. I'll organize a boat for you the moment you're ready to leave. We'll get *Baby Dolphin* back to Mora too, of course.'

There was a long silence. All that broke it was the crackle of logs in the fire and the wash of the sea below them. Hetty looked at the old man. The question had been fretting inside her and now was the time to ask it.

'Tell me what you meant,' she said. 'When I told you I've brought Rosa home, and you said, "Perhaps you have". What did you mean?'

Tor smiled at her.

'My wife's name is Marita,' he said. 'Rosa was my daughter.'

The old man looked at the figure in the bed.

'I think my wife went off to find Rosa and bring her home. And perhaps she did. Perhaps you both did.'

He turned to Hetty again.

'Forgive me,' he said. 'You've brought my wife back to me. You don't need the burden of pretending to be my lost daughter as well.'

The door opened and a small face peeped round.

197

'Come in, Per,' said Kristina.

The boy walked nervously up to the bed and it took Hetty a moment to realize that he was avoiding her eyes.

'What's wrong?' she said to him.

'Don't be angry with me.'

'Why should I be angry with you?'

'I left your boat,' said Per, 'and I promised I'd look after her. But Sten and the other men told me I had to. They said—'

'It's all right, Per,' said Hetty quickly. 'Your father's explained everything. He's told me they're going to give her a new mast and sail and clean her up. You're not in trouble at all. I'm really grateful to you for helping me. I didn't know what to do when I arrived at the quay and I was really nervous, and you came straight up and took my hand and welcomed me. Thank you.'

The boy looked at her doubtfully.

'Come and sit here,' she said.

'You're holding Grandmother's hand.'

'I know,' she said. 'Do you think that's all right?'

'I used to hold her hand,' said Per. 'Especially when she couldn't find things and got frightened.'

'Come and sit on the bed,' said Hetty, 'and hold my other hand.'

Per climbed next to her on the bed and took her hand. She turned her head to look at the woman, lying there as still as ever, her breaths just audible in the silent room.

'Marita,' she whispered.

She felt a hand on her shoulder and knew it was Tor's.

'I wish I'd known her name,' she said. 'When we were on Mora, and in the boat. I'd like to have spoken it to her.'

'You still can,' he said.

'Marita,' she whispered again.

The silence deepened around them, and around the bed. An hour later no one had spoken. They sat in the same positions, aware of each other and the figure in the bed. At some point Hetty remembered Aidan nursing the fire and lighting fresh candles. Later she felt a hand on her arm. She looked up with a start to find herself lying on the side of the bed with Per curled up against her, and both of them leaning in to the motionless figure of Marita. The hand squeezed her arm and she saw Kristina bending over her.

'Aidan moved you,' she whispered. 'You were falling asleep on the edge of the bed. So was Per. So he carried you both over here and laid you down.'

'Thank you,' she murmured.

She looked down at Per and put an arm over him. Kristina returned to the other side of the bed and sat down in the same chair as before. Tor and Aidan were still sitting there, but the old man was nodding. She looked at Marita again, willing the eyes to open, just as she'd done in the boat, but they did not. The next time she woke, it was to Per's voice.

'Hetty,' he was saying, 'wake up.'

She opened her eyes to see him peering up at her. He said no more but she knew at once from the atmosphere that everything had changed. Tor, Aidan, and Kristina were all standing, and another man was with them, a bearded man. Tor caught her eye.

'This is Doctor Yannick,' he said quietly.

No one spoke further. Hetty stayed on the bed but sat up, aware of Per clinging to her. She slipped an arm round him and peered down at Marita. The breathing was regular but the whole tone of it was different. She wasn't sure how she knew this was the end. She reached under the sheet and felt for Marita's hand. She found it and closed it inside her own, whispering.

'Marita, Marita . . .'

The breathing went on.

In, out, in, out.

Hetty squeezed the hand gently. There was no response. She leaned closer to Marita's face, aware of Tor doing the same from the other side.

'Mother,' she said softly.

She sensed a movement in the eyes, just the smallest outward glance, then they were still, and all that was left was the breathing.

In, out, in, out.

In . . .

And then nothing.

It was evening.

# *Chapter 28*

She slept through into the night, a strange, fitful sleep with dreams of the sea, and then she woke, some time in the early hours. A frosty moon was cutting into the room from the window overlooking the harbour. She sat up in bed and looked about her.

Most of the room was dark but the glow from the window illuminated a chair close to the bed. She saw that her clothes had been taken away and in their place was a pile of new ones, neatly folded. Even in this uncertain light she could see that they were nothing like the clothes she normally wore. She swung out of bed and examined them.

Prettier by far. She'd never had such beautiful clothes. She placed them back on the chair, then caught sight of something on the bedside table: something that glinted at her. She reached out and her hand closed over the sea glass.

She picked it up and held it high. It glinted again, though she was holding it in darkness. She moved it round so that the moon-glow fell upon it. The light passed through like a river. She stared at the surface, searching for the images that had been there. But it was clear. Just a piece of glass.

As Grandy would say.

She closed it inside her hand, remembering Marita's tiny fist, then stood up and walked over to the window. Below her was a small garden, bordered by trees but with a gap at the bottom where a path seemed to lead down in the direction of the town. Below that was the harbour, and the sea beyond, glistening in the night.

No sounds came from below, or from the room itself. She gazed over the water, searching the surface. It was still and smooth. She shivered suddenly and pulled on the dressing gown, then, on an impulse, turned and slipped out of the room.

The house was dark, but she found her way easily to the main door, and out round the side of the building to the gate into the garden. She pushed it open and stepped through, the grass moist and cold against her bare feet. A chill was rising from the sea and merging with the cool of the night.

She pulled the dressing gown more tightly around her and wandered across the garden towards the gap she had seen from her window. It did indeed open onto a path and she followed this through shrubs and saplings to a wooden fence just a short way down. It was only chest height and she leaned on it, breathing in the air from the sea.

From here she had a clear, unbroken view of the water and both sides of the bay. The moon was falling upon the headland over to the right, and she could see the foaming white of the seas around the lower rocks of the Three Spears. Apart from that, nothing seemed to move.

'Hetty,' said a voice.

She saw a figure edging towards her from the right.

'It's only me,' said Tor.

The old man stopped beside her, breathing slowly.

'I hope I didn't startle you,' he said.

She looked at him. He was smiling at her in the night, but there was weariness in his face, and the pain she had noticed from the first moment she saw him. He turned heavily and leaned on the fence, and she did the same, and they stood there for some minutes, contemplating the sea in silence.

'I couldn't sleep,' he said eventually, 'so I came outside. I was standing over there.'

He pointed to the right.

'I've been here for an hour or so. I didn't hear you come out. You're sure I didn't startle you just now?'

'No, I'm fine.'

She glanced at him, but he was still gazing over the sea.

'You must be thinking of Mora,' he said.

She didn't answer.

'We'll get you back,' he went on. 'Aidan's going to arrange a boat. If you were from Broma or Styr or even Brinda, there would be no problem. We get lots of boats from those islands and any one of them could take you home, but Mora is different. You're so far away. You're even further than Faerde. We get very few boats from out there. We know Mackie, of course. He has been here many times over the years, and he and Sten are good friends, but we know he trades direct with Ivan in Brinda, so that's probably why he hasn't been here for a while.'

The old man shook his head.

'I'm so sorry you've lost *The Pride of Mora*. She was a beauty. I'd have been proud to have built such a boat.'

'They started building another one,' said Hetty, 'but lots of the timber we had was rotten, so Mackie's building a smaller boat just to get a message to Brinda to ask for help. I was going to tell you in case there's anything you can do from here.'

Tor looked round at her.

'Aidan's told me he wants to take you home personally, so he can carry timber for Mackie at the same time. I'll get him to offer tools and equipment as well. But most important of all, he can get you back to your mother and father.'

'I live with my grandmother.'

'Just your grandmother?'

'Yes,' said Hetty.

The old man studied her for a moment, then simply nodded.

'Then we'll get you back to your grandmother,' he said.

And he turned back to stare over the water again. They gazed at it together for a few minutes, then Tor went on, quietly.

'The sea takes so many, Hetty,' he said. 'It took a brother of mine too, many years ago, and men I've sailed with. But you know all about loss, living on Mora.'

'What was Rosa like?'

'She looked like you,' said Tor, 'as I told you earlier, and she had a quality you have. A kind of independence, and something else. She carried the other world with her. You understand what I mean? She got that from Marita. They were both the same. They saw and heard things I know nothing of. I don't know if you're like that. Perhaps you are.'

Hetty fingered the sea glass again.

'Do you . . . do you still grieve for Rosa?'

'Of course I do,' said Tor, 'and I've been grieving for Marita almost as long. Because I lost her too the day Rosa went over the side.'

He looked round again.

'But I'll get through, Hetty,' he said, 'and I'll feel even better when I know you're back with your grandmother. Come on. You need to sleep and I should do the same.'

They started to walk up the path towards the house, and as they did so, she heard the whispers from the sea far below her. She stopped and looked back. The lustre was gone from the surface of the water and all was dark again. She realized suddenly that Tor had stopped too. She turned and saw him watching her with a smile.

'Rosa used to do that,' he said.

'Do what?'

'Stare at the sea like she was listening to something it was telling her. I've seen Marita do it too.' The old man touched her on the arm. 'Goodnight, Hetty. Come in when you're ready.'

And he trudged off across the garden and round the side of the house. Hetty turned back to the sea. The darkness was still there, not just in the water but over the headland and in the sky, and even the little town itself. She walked up to the house, made her way in through the door, and back to her room. The moon-glow had not returned and all was sombre. She sat on the edge of the bed and studied the sea glass. It was as dark as the ocean, as dark as all things.

She placed it on the table, climbed into bed, and cried. It was only much later that she realized who she had been crying for. She pictured her mother's face, and her father's face, as she had always imagined them both, and let the movement of the night fold over them, and over her.

But sleep did not come. She wanted it to. She yearned for rest, and freedom from these reflections, which had only ever brought her pain. She was picturing Mora now, and Grandy, and recognizing for the first time and with a stab of guilt that there was something she had never considered in all her years of wondering: that Grandy must have grieved too, though she had never shown it.

The night moved on, pulling her into sleep and out again, the images following her in dreams and in waking, and then it was first light, and she could hear gulls mewing far away. She lay there, thinking of Moon Cottage, and her tiny room; and then she fell asleep again. The next time she woke, it was to a touch on her arm, and the sense of someone close: someone small.

'Hetty,' said Per, 'wake up.'

She saw the boy leaning over her, his eyes wide. Kristina was standing behind him, the sun in the window bright upon both of them, and there were voices outside the door and in the town.

'What time is it?' said Hetty.

'Noon,' said Kristina.

'Noon?'

'Yes. You've slept and slept, but we had to wake you.'

'There's news,' said Per.

Hetty looked at him and saw he was holding the sea glass. He noticed her watching and put it quickly back on the table.

'I'm sorry,' he said. 'I didn't mean to touch it.'

She sat up in bed and took the sea glass.

'I'm really sorry,' said Per.

She smiled and put it back in the boy's hand.

'You keep it, Per.'

'But—'

'I want you to.' She closed his fingers round it. 'I really do. It's yours for ever now. What's your news?'

'There's a boat coming into the harbour.'

'A boat?'

'Yes,' said Kristina, 'and we all recognize her. It's Ivan's boat from Brinda. *The Northern Star.* And Sten and Aidan have spotted Mackie on board.'

'Mackie!'

'And some other men from Mora.'

Hetty flung back the covers and started to scramble out of bed. Kristina took her arm and stopped her.

'That's not all,' she said. 'There's someone else with them.'

'Who?'

'We don't know for sure,' said Kristina, 'but we can guess.'

# Chapter 29

'Grandy!' said Hetty.

She threw her arms round her grandmother at the top of the quayside steps.

'Hetty, you brave silly girl.'

Hetty held on, unable to let go. Grandy's body shook for a moment, but then she drew back. Hetty looked up at her, then round at the quayside and harbour wall, crowded again, as they had been on her arrival, and then at *The Northern Star* moored below.

A fine vessel, larger even than *The Pride of Mora*. Mackie was standing in the bow with Hal, Karl, and Rory, all four waving to her. The deck of the boat was packed with men, some from Haga—she recognized Sten and two of his crew—and others, she supposed, from Brinda. A burly man wandered forward to join Mackie in the bows.

'That's Ivan,' said Grandy. 'He owns *The Northern Star*.'

But Hetty couldn't answer. All she wanted was to pull Grandy away and be alone with her. She felt someone take her hand and knew who it was without looking.

'Who's this?' said Grandy, smiling down.

'My friend Per,' she said.

'Hello, Per. I'm Grandy.'

'Hello,' said Per.

'And this is Tor,' said Hetty. 'Per's grandfather.'

Tor stepped forward and bowed to Grandy.

'He was married to Marita,' said Hetty.

'Marita?'

'Yes.'

She saw a question appear in Grandy's face; and then vanish.

'I understand,' said Grandy slowly, 'and is Marita . . . ?'

'She died yesterday,' said Tor.

'I'm sorry.'

'It was meant to be,' said the old man. 'I'm only glad she was with her family at the end.'

He looked at Hetty, but said no more. Aidan and Kristina arrived and Hetty found herself making more introductions. Out of the corner of her eye she saw Mackie and the others coming ashore.

'Grandy,' she said, 'how did you get to Brinda without a boat?'

'We had a boat.'

'But—'

'We took one of the rowing boats.'

'Are you serious?'

'We had no choice,' said Grandy, 'so we took old Per's boat.'

'That's a wreck!'

'You're telling me,' said Grandy. 'I spent most of my time baling. But it was the only boat with space for four rowers.'

'That was mad.'

Grandy shrugged.

'No more mad than what you did. It was Mackie's doing. When I read your note and told him you were trying to reach Brinda in *Baby Dolphin*, he called a meeting straightaway and asked for volunteers to row with him.'

'I wouldn't have thought there'd be any,' said Hetty, 'not for me.'

'Everybody volunteered,' said Grandy. 'Every hand went up at the meeting, even Harold's. It pulled us together, made us realize what's important. Mackie had as many people as he wanted, so he picked the four strongest men, including himself. Tam was desperate to come, as you can imagine. He pretty much begged his father, but Mackie said no. He didn't think it fair on Isla if she lost both of them. So he chose Hal, Karl, and Rory to go with him.'

'And you.'

'Well, they were pretty much stuck with me,' said Grandy. 'I told Mackie I was coming whether they liked it or not. They didn't want me at first but I think they were glad in the end. I took the helm and navigated, and did the baling and gave them food and water, and although they complained that I weighed too much, I think I did some good.'

Tor shook his head.

'That was more than brave,' he said. 'To row all the way from Mora to Brinda in a small, leaky boat, and in those seas. And there was a storm, Hetty said. It must have hit you too.'

'It did.'

'Hetty lost her mast in it and got blown far off course. She only just limped into Haga.'

'I need to hear all this,' said Grandy. She put an arm round Hetty. 'When you're ready to tell me.'

'But you haven't finished your own story.'

'It's soon told,' said Grandy. 'We battled through the storm and made it to Brinda. Ivan told us you hadn't turned up, so we set off in *The Northern Star* to look for you. We thought there was just a chance we might find you somewhere in the seas round Brinda. It didn't occur to any of us that you'd make it to Haga. We only came here out of a last desperate hope.'

Mackie and the others were now walking up the steps to the quay. Hetty let go of Grandy and ran down to meet them. They saw her coming and stopped halfway.

'Mackie!' she said.

And she tumbled into him.

'Easy,' he said, lifting her off her feet.

He put her back down on the step and she hugged the others, and then Mackie again.

'I never thought you'd come looking for me,' she said.

'Why wouldn't we?' said Mackie. 'You're one of our own, Hetty. And we always look after our own.'

He picked her up again, carried her to the top of the stairs and put her down once more. Tor walked forward with Aidan and Kristina, and Grandy, and Per. Hetty took the boy's hand again and squeezed it. He looked up at her, and she saw he was holding the sea glass in his other hand. Tor and Mackie embraced each other and drew apart.

'It's good to see you again, Mackie,' said Tor, 'after so many years.'

'Mackie,' said Hetty, 'it was Tor's wife who was with us on Mora. Her name was Marita.'

Mackie looked at her.

'Was?' he said.

'She died yesterday,' said Tor.

Mackie turned back to him.

'I'm so sorry to hear that,' he said, 'and I wish I'd known she was your wife. But I don't think I ever saw her on my voyages here. I was always tied up with Sten and the others doing business.'

'That's of no importance,' said Tor. 'What matters is that Hetty brought her home.'

'Yes, indeed.' Mackie glanced at Hetty. 'Well done, girl.'

He turned to Aidan.

'Good to see you again, Aidan.'

'And you, Mackie.'

'Is this your wife?'

'Yes,' said Aidan. 'This is Kristina, and this is my son Per.'

Mackie nodded to both, then indicated Karl, Hal, and Rory.

210

'You remember these three, I'm sure.'

'Of course we do,' said Aidan. 'You're all very welcome.'

'Tor,' said Hetty suddenly, 'when is the service for Marita?'

'Later this afternoon,' said Tor. He looked hard at her. 'How did you know I was thinking of Marita just now?'

Hetty said nothing. The old man shook his head.

'You're so like Rosa, Hetty. And so like Marita.'

'Can Grandy and I come to the ceremony?' she said.

'Of course you can.'

'Us too?' said Mackie. 'If it's not an intrusion, we'd like to pay our respects. Only I'm afraid we have no proper clothes.'

'Come as you are,' said Tor. 'We would love to see you there. And Ivan and his crew if they wish to come. The whole town will be at Marita's farewell and no one will mind how you are dressed.'

The service turned out as the old man had described. The congregation not only filled the church but spilt through the open door into the graveyard and out into the lane. After the ceremony was over and Marita had been laid to rest, Hetty walked out along the headland with Grandy, leaving the others behind. They did not speak as they made their way to the point. They stopped a few feet back from the edge and stared down at the water licking against the Three Spears. Hetty took a long breath.

'Grandy,' she began, 'I've thought really hard about this and—'

'I know,' said Grandy. 'You're not coming back to Mora. You want to try to make a life here on the mainland.'

Hetty stared at her.

'How did you know that?'

'I just did,' said Grandy.

Hetty felt the tears start. Grandy held out her arms.

'Come here, girl. Give me a hug.'

Hetty held her close, crying quietly.

'There's nothing on Mora I want now, Grandy,' she said. 'It's like . . . the island's not part of me any more.'

'I know,' said Grandy. 'I understand.'

'Are you angry with me?'

'Of course not.'

Grandy drew back.

'Dry your eyes, Hetty,' she said. 'I'm not angry with you at all. I'm proud of you, more proud than you'll ever know. And I'll tell you something else: your mother and father would be proud too.'

They turned back to the harbour and saw Tor walking towards them with little Per.

'I've been speaking to Ivan and Mackie,' the old man said, 'and they've decided to set off this evening. The tide's perfect and if conditions stay as they are, *The Northern Star* should be somewhere close to Brinda by dusk tomorrow. You can then spend the night on Brinda and travel on to Mora the following day. Ivan says he can carry *Baby Dolphin*. She'll fit nicely amidships, even with the timber they're loading.'

'I'm not going back to Mora,' said Hetty.

Tor gave her a questioning look.

'I've made up my mind,' she said, 'and I've told Grandy. She'll be going back with Mackie and the others, but I'll be staying here.'

'No,' said Grandy.

Hetty looked round at her.

'I won't be going back either, sweetheart,' said Grandy. 'I made a promise to your mother and father after they drowned. I'd rather have made it to their faces but never mind. I made it in the chapel and told them I'd never desert you as long as I have breath. So I'm not going back to Mora either. I don't know where we'll live or what we'll do, but we'll find a way to get you started in the world.'

'You'll live with us,' said Per. 'Won't they, Grandfather?'

'Of course they will,' said Tor.

'We can't let you do that,' said Grandy.

Tor was silent for a moment, then he looked at Hetty.

'Is that what you'd like, Hetty?' he said. 'To stay with us for as long as you want until you find your way? And to have your grandmother with you?' He paused. 'Because that is what we would like.'

Hetty bit her lip.

'I would like it too,' she said.

The evening tide was well under way as *The Northern Star*, now laden with timber, set off from the quay. The people of Haga had again crowded the waterfront, but Hetty found a place at the outermost point of the harbour mouth, where the sea beckoned to the approaching boat. Only Per was with her—the others were watching from the quay—and she was glad of his company. It had been hard to say goodbye to the men. The boat drew nearer and Mackie saw her at last at the top of the wall. He walked into the bow and peered up at her.

'Mackie?' she said. 'Can you tell Tam something?'

'Of course.'

'It's really important.'

'What is it?'

She hesitated.

'Tell him I'm sorry, Mackie. Please tell him that. And say . . .'

She stopped, thinking hard. The boat moved on, picking up speed. She felt a sudden urgency to find more words, and better ones—but Mackie spoke first.

'He'll be all right, Hetty.'

She looked down at him gratefully.

'I promise he will,' said Mackie.

He smiled at her.

'Be happy.'

And *The Northern Star* passed beyond the harbour mouth and glided towards the headland. Hetty stood there and watched until the boat had rounded The Three Spears and disappeared from view, then she sat down on a large bollard, made space for Per to sit next to her, and put an arm round him; and they stared over the sea in silence.

Dusk fell.

She glanced over her shoulder and scanned the quay and harbour walls. They were empty now of people but figures were moving further up the town and she could see lights on in the windows. Tor's house up on the rise was bright and clear. She felt Per shiver and looked down at him.

'You're cold,' she said.

'No, I'm not.'

But his voice betrayed him. He shivered again.

'Why don't you go back to the house?' she said.

He leaned into her.

'I'm going to stay here,' she said, 'but just for a bit. You run back and tell them I'm coming. Can you do that?'

He stood up.

'Thank you, Per.'

She watched him run off down the harbour wall and up the lane into the town, then she turned back to the sea. It was losing all sense of day now as first the grey, then the black reclaimed it, but she sat there even so, heedless of the chill, and watched, and thought, and searched. But the water was like the sea glass now: empty of all she wanted. Yet perhaps it no longer mattered, she thought. Perhaps there was no need to keep on searching; just a need to move on. She stood up and stared one last time into the sea, and then she heard it, whispering back: her name, just once; and she turned away, carrying the sound with her.

Tim Bowler is one of the UK's most compelling and original writers for teenagers. He was born in Leigh-on-Sea and after studying Swedish at university, he worked in forestry, the timber trade, teaching, and translating before becoming a full-time writer. He lives with his wife in a small village in Devon and his workroom is an old stone outhouse known to friends as 'Tim's Bolthole'.

Tim has written eighteen books and won fifteen awards, including the prestigious Carnegie Medal for *River Boy*, and his provocative *BLADE* series is being hailed as a groundbreaking work of fiction. He has been described by the *Sunday Telegraph* as 'the master of the psychological thriller' and by the *Independent* as 'one of the truly individual voices in British teenage fiction'.

www.timbowler.co.uk